STARLESS MIDNIGHT

STARLESS MIDNIGHT

Lynn Garthwaite

Published 2020
Printed in the United States of America
ISBN: 978-1-952976-02-5
Library of Congress Control Number: 2020942275

Cover Design & Interior Book Design: Ann Aubitz

For more information contact:
Kirk House Publishers
1250 E 115th Street
Burnsville, MN 55337

STARLESS MIDNIGHT

Lynn Garthwaite

Published 2020
Printed in the United States of America
ISBN: 978-1-952976-02-5
Library of Congress Control Number: 2020942275

Cover Design & Interior Book Design: Ann Aubitz

For more information contact:
Kirk House Publishers
1250 E 115th Street
Burnsville, MN 55337

Acknowledgments

My special thanks to the wisdom and talents of Amanda Gronhovd, Minnesota State Archaeologist. I appreciate your help describing the details of what a murder victim would look like when uncovered after 40 years in, let's call it, "an uncommon environment."

And to Brad Hanson, owner of Profinishers Auto Body in Prior Lake, MN. When I need auto body work done, or someone who can describe the best way to bash in a car's gas tank to blow things up, of course I go to Brad. Thanks buddy! www.profinishers.com

And the face-saving Claudette Hegel, copyeditor extraordinaire. Thanks for your superhuman patience with an author who keeps making the same mistakes no matter how many times you gently point them out. Passive voice? Never heard of it.

Something else super helpful to authors? Beta Readers. Thank you to Karen Anderson, Helen Lapakko, and Kathryn Holmes. The best feed-back and nudges I could have asked for.

I dedicate this book to my two sons, Ryan and Scott, who, in spite of a mom who does not possess a single guesstimation gene and whose scathingly brilliant ideas are usually more like laughingly odd moments, turned out to be people I am in awe of. I love you!

Prologue

Three years ago

His heart pounded in his ears. *Run. Keep going. The forest is thicker here. Where's the path? I can't find a way through.*

His right leg strained to keep up the pace, but his left one, the one they hit with a bat, was weakened, failing. Deep scratches from the small, sharp buckthorn shrubs left blood running down his arms. His ebony skin shone with sweat. *Gotta move faster. Get past that ridge.*

Did the dusk turn to night while he ran, or had the forest become so dense it blotted out the last of the sun?

He was in trouble. *My life. My life.* The men who followed screamed his name, their voices ugly with hate, relishing the hunt. Their boots pounded. His boots dragged. His eyes searched for some place to take cover. *Hide. Let them pass. I can't. No time. No place safe.* Sharp pains shot up his shins and his lungs were done. *Nothing's working any more.* His legs buckled with exhaustion. His will alone would not last long enough to carry him to safety. *Too old now. Too old.*

His mind started to settle. To bargain. Should he just lie down and let them send him to meet God? Would he be able to endure the torture he knew would come before the final shot? His fingers reached to wipe away the sweat stinging his eyes, but the blood that had run in rivulets to his hands just mixed with the sweat. Sticky. With blurred vision he pushed his way through branches that scraped his forehead and tore at his face.

They were close now. *Oh, dear God, please send angels to protect my beloved Sonya.* Would she ever know why he wasn't coming home?

Chapter 1

Today

Jadey looked ahead on the highway and felt an involuntary shiver pulse through her in spite of the June heat angling on her windshield. The town was still out of sight, but old memories of fear and anger hit her full in the gut.

"Well, this is a good start." Jadey laughed without amusement. The crunch of loose gravel was loud under her tires as she rolled onto the shoulder of the road. She twisted the key, a moot point since the engine had died one hundred yards back and it was only through the grace of the rolling tires that she made it off the highway. Staring at a cornfield stretching half-a-mile to the south, she sighed. You had only eighty-three miles to go, Jadey Evans, and you made it seventy-nine. One more gallon of gas would have gotten you there. A minute ago, she was sailing down the highway, singing along to her favorite Jason Mraz song, and now she sat looking at June corn.

With one hearty "freaking dammit" she straightened up, threw open the door and pulled herself out of the car.

The summer air was dusty, and hot, and smelled vaguely of manure from a source Jadey recognized. Sure enough, farmland as far as she could see, but somewhere past the corn, the soft lowing sounds of cattle brought a brief smile. Sweat began beading on her caramel-colored skin.

Reaching back into her car, she fumbled for her cell phone. "You've got to be kidding me!" No bars and a quick attempt to get a dial tone confirmed her worst fears. She looked at her feet where her favorite burgundy-and-gray side-strap sandals were already dusty, and then looked at the road stretching ahead of her. No signs of civilization as far as her eyes could see. Those sandals were not going to get her into town without some major hurt. Jadey groaned. To dig through the back seat, jammed with all her belongings, to try to find her tennis-shoes, seemed like a job that would take an hour. It was just too hot.

Traffic had been light, but not non-existent, so Jadey decided her best bet was to flag down a passing car to get a ride. Needing help wasn't her best look. She spent her lifetime, all twenty-eight years, trying to prove she didn't need help from anyone. She fussed for a while, wondering what would be the proper way to attract assistance but not a predator. She had no patience for women who feign helplessness and flaunt a sexual come-on, but a look down at her cotton, tangerine-hued sundress, now starting to cling with sweat in all the wrong places, made her uneasy.

Her luck appeared to have improved when she saw a squad car pull in behind her. Relieved she wouldn't have to navigate a discussion with a random stranger, Jadey relaxed, just now noticing the muscles in her neck were rigid and her shoulders tense.

But, oh boy. Her mouth twitched with a hint of a smile as a pair of long legs followed by some rarified oh-my-goodness pulled itself out of the cruiser. With the sun at his back, she couldn't quite see the face coming toward her, but her gaze wasn't locked onto his face.

"Ma'am" the officer said as he neared.

Jadey laughed. At twenty-eight, the idea of being called "Ma'am" was funny. Even her own mom bristled at being called "Ma'am."

"Can I see your ID?"

"I just ran out of gas," she said. "Do I need to prove my identity for that?"

"Routine Ma'am. Even serial killers run out of gas sometimes." Jadey noticed the officer testing her car's trunk to make sure it was latched. His eyes scanned the inside of the car, sizing up the backseat stuffed with bags and household goods.

"Do you have many female serial killers come along County Road Five, Officer? Or who head for Twinktown, Wisconsin? Population 13,000?"

"Not many. Probably due."

Jadey stared at him. Does this man have a sense of humor? Or sweat glands? He didn't seem fazed by the heat.

"How do you stay so cool?" she asked as she reached into the front seat and pulled her billfold from her purse. As she handed him her ID, Jadey looked at the name sewn onto his uniform. *Dillanian, G.* His badge indicated he was a sergeant. And now that she was at a different angle, she noted to herself that the face matched the "oh my goodness" of the rest of him.

He ignored her question, but eventually spoke, finally looking up from the ID in his hand. "The town up ahead is actually Twin Station. And the population is closer to 25,000."

"Twenty-five thousand? Crap! You know how when you live in a town as a kid, you attach a variety of nicknames to it? Twinktown, Toonville, Twinkletoes.... But I'm glad to hear it's growing."

Dillanian's eyes scanned the picture on the ID again and then moved to her face, making the comparison. Jadey screwed up her face in a cartoonish grin, but failed to get a smile from him. She waited for the question, are you Caucasian or Black? It seemed to be the first thing every bi-racial person is asked.

"Jadai Orion Evans?" He bungled the pronunciation of her first name.

Jadey sighed. "Pronounced almost like Jedi, but with an emphasis on the 'eye" ending. Let's just stipulate my mother was a wannabe hippie, okay?"

"Stipulate. Are you a lawyer?"

"Not even a little close. Okay, my name was created for the purpose of giving me the initials J-O-E. Joe was the love of my mom's life, and also probably my dad."

Dillanian ignored the extra piece of information, but pushed the point. "Jadai? Did she just make that up?"

"As far as I know. I said she was a wannabe hippie. Everyone calls me Jadey."

"Says here your hair is blonde."

Jadey subconsciously ran her hand through her shoulder-length, brown hair, soft with curls framing her face. "Last year. Right now, I'm thinking about red. The

DMV won't let me change my ID whenever I change my hair color."

"You asked them?"

"No, I'm psychic." She rolled her eyes. "Listen, I just ran out of gas, and I promise I'm not a serial killer. Can you help me?"

"Stay here please."

Dillanian walked to his squad car and sat in the front seat with one foot on the pavement through the open door. Jadey could see him pick up the radio and speak into it, reading off the information from her driver's license. After a moment he set down the handset, exited the car and went to the trunk of the squad. When he came around, Jadey relaxed her tense shoulders when she saw he had pulled out a gas can.

"I appreciate it," she told him as he unscrewed her gas cap and began pouring gas into her tank. "I'll pay it forward and do something nice for someone else today."

"No need Ma'am. It's the 'serve' part of Protect and Serve. First one's on us. If you run out of gas again, we take your first-born child." He handed her back her ID, his face neutral.

"If I ever have one, I'll be sure to keep my tank full at all times."

The two looked at each other, Jadey searching for any sign of a sense of humor in the sergeant. His expression gave away nothing. Eventually he tipped his hat and walked back to his squad car.

As Jadey pulled away, she looked in her rearview mirror to see Sergeant Dillanian writing something in his notebook, a scowl on his face. Ahead of her was the town of Twin Station, and Jadey faced it with a mixture of curiosity and dread.

Chapter 2

With only a couple of wrong turns, Jadey found herself staring at the house where she lived until she was fourteen. A Victorian style structure, it showcased a large front porch and a classic steep roof and asymmetrical vertical features. Most of it seemed still in decent shape, although the years had taken its toll on some of the siding and eaves. Chipped paint and the signs of natural wear took some charm from the quaintness she remembered as a child. The garden in front appeared well cared for, with only some scraggly weeds breaking through in the month since her Grandma Ellie died.

Jadey hadn't seen the house in fourteen years. She knew every inch of it and was personally responsible for some of the repairs her grandma was forced to make. Jadey and her mom had been back for the funeral, but her mom refused to let them come near the house of her own youth. Jadey knew better than to push it. The quiet, white house with fading green shutters seemed to have some kind of power over her mother, a history Jadey had yet to learn.

She turned to look down the block, remembering some of the neighbors. None of the houses were particularly close. Each sat on about five acres of property, so the yards were big and the wild spaces in-between became a part of the landscaping. To her right, she remembered the Sheridans, an older couple who regularly visited Grandma Ellie. Beyond the Sheridans', a blue one-story house that kept changing owners. Although she couldn't think of the last names of any of the people who lived there, a quick memory flashed of a little girl whose family stayed only a short time. The girl had skin the same color as her own, and the two young neighbors had shyly made a brief friendship. Why can't I think of her name? Jadey's face twisted, trying to remember.

To her left stood the house where the Billings once lived. She knew from her grandma's stories that after Gladys Billings finally died, the house stayed vacant, now owned by the bank because none of the Billings kids had an interest in coming back to claim it. Beyond the Billings house, the homes stood closer together, on smaller pieces of property. Those streets, set up in square grids throughout the town, were the more typical residential area. Everything in the area eventually connected to the main street and retail parts of downtown.

Her eyes returned to the house she knew as a child. Clearly no one had come to tidy up, or to even give the appearance the house was being cared for, and Jadey felt a little guilty it had taken her this long to come. A garden hose still zig-zagged across part of the front-yard, its head in a flower bed where her grandma had last let it flow. A shovel leaned up against the side of the house next to an area where it appeared her grandma had been thinning the yellow Stella D'Oro daylilies that threatened to overtake the petite cornflowers. Competing colors and styles throughout the bed made Jadey smile, and she could picture her grandma taking cuttings of all of them to brighten up her home. She walked around to the back door and hesitated. The keys were in her hand, but her arm tensed up, her brain unable or unwilling to insert them into the lock. She stood there for a moment, and then made up an excuse to delay entry. Walking back to the front, Jadey grabbed the shovel and other gardening implements and carried them to the shed in back.

Even the shed brought back memories. Grandma was a putterer, and her shed was as much of a happy place for her as her kitchen. She had warned Jadey away from the shed, though. "Too many sharp tools in here, sweetie. I want you to stay out of the shed. Nothing but trouble for you in here." Grandma Ellie. Her fun buddy, and always a protector. Jadey pulled the big door open and wedged the tools into the crowded space inside.

When she turned to look again at the home where she spent the first half of her life, her hand subconsciously went to her stomach, where her apprehension registered as a familiar twinge.

The back door opened directly into the old kitchen, where apparently nothing had changed since she lived there. A beat-up butcher block counter showed signs of burns and stains from decades of use. The appliances were the same as she remembered. The cabinets were still the golden oak boxes, but some of the doors now hung slightly askew, as if even the hinges had aged past their prime.

The house was stone silent and she wondered if it had died right along with Grandma. Scenes played in her head of Grandma pulling out a sheet of cookies and filling the room with a wonderful aroma.

●●●●●

"Yay! Peanut Butter Cookies!"

"You know they're my favorites too. I think you inherited your cookie love from me, Jadey."

Country western music played on the ancient radio on the counter.

"Mom says that I inherited your stubborn side too. Am I stubborn, Grandma?"

"Ridiculous. Remember this, little sweetheart. You're strong-minded. Persistent."

"I like persis ... what's that word?"

"Persistent. It means you know what you want and you're not afraid to go after it."

●●●●●

Persistent. Grandma had been right. Jadey had grown into a persistent woman. Stubborn, too.

But those scenes faded and her mind replaced them with different memories; the other truths of this home. Arguments, accusations, and recriminations also hung in the air, as if time had not let those moments fade away.

"Oh, Grandma. Why did you have to die on me? And what exactly did you leave me?"

She looked around the room, opening cupboard doors and drawers, wiping something greasy off the counter with her finger and grabbing a paper towel to clean it off. She slowly wandered through the other rooms, memories flooding back from the last time she was there – fourteen years ago. Not much had changed, but she shivered in spite of the heat, thinking about how wrong everything had gone.

Tears came to her eyes when she noticed pictures of her, from toddler years all the way up to her first book signing event, a year ago.

No pictures of her mother. Of course not.

She stole a glance up the staircase, leading to the bedrooms, trying to avoid looking at the bottom of the steps where a neighbor had found her grandma's body. How did she know to look? Were they still close enough that they checked up on each other? Had the neighbor heard something? How long had she lain there, alone, before someone came?

She took a few steps up and then stopped. Yep, there was the creaky stair. A memory flashed in her mind about how she learned to navigate the old stairs, knowing when to step to one side or another to avoid the scary squeaks. It had been like a game to her, making the stairs a mini-maze of steps.

From where she stood on the third step, she could see the landing at the top of the stairs was dark. Clouds had moved in, blocking the natural light from the upstairs windows. A room had belonged to her up there, once upon a time, and along with it the feeling of belonging somewhere. A feeling she never completely captured since. This had been home, although it was a home of fractured moments. Her own mother battled mostly-unseen demons for as long as Jadey could remember, although one of her demons was always in plain view: Grandma.

How odd that Jadey's relationship with her grandma was such a polar opposite of the one the two adult women shared. Grandma Ellie was a friend, confidant, and fellow-adventurer for Jadey, but she was a lightning rod for Trish, her own daughter.

"If only walls could talk," Jadey said aloud on the staircase. "And maybe answer a few questions."

She paused for a second, letting the thought sit there, and then found herself inhaling a deep breath and shouting as loud as she could, screaming at the ceiling.

"I'd like a few answers – please!"

She jumped when a series of thuds at the door followed her outburst. Her hand shot to her face, suddenly warm, and she feared her screech may have been heard by some unknown person. Then curiosity about who could possibly be knocking on the door made her forget her embarrassment. She returned to the bottom of the stairs, walked through the small living room, and up to the door. She paused as she reached for the deadbolt.

With the door open, she experienced a split-second flash of familiarity, leaving her to wonder if this could be someone she knew. The man at the door looked to be about her age, with jeans and a t-shirt christened with generous sprays of motor oil and a few other stains she couldn't identify. His hair was a little long, hanging below his ears and probably just finger combed right before she opened the door. His face was adorable, and his smile was tentative.

"Jadey? I heard you came back."

"Wait. Doug? Doug Baylor? For goodness sake, what are you doing here?"

Doug stood awkwardly at the open door, looking over her shoulder at the inside of the house. "I heard from Greg you were back in town. I couldn't believe it. When your grandma died, I pretty much gave up hope of seeing you again. You were at the funeral, but you and your mom left so fast I didn't get a chance to talk to you."

Jadey suddenly realized he was still standing outside the door, so she stepped aside and gestured for him to come in.

"My mom couldn't get out of here fast enough. We definitely were not going to be lingering in Twin Station, apparently. Who's Greg? I don't remember any Greg from school."

Doug crossed the threshold and took a long look around. "Greg Dillanian. Police sergeant. I just saw him in town and he said Ellie Evans' kid was in town. I wasn't sure if he meant your mom or you – so I came right over to see for myself."

Jadey laughed, noting to herself how unlikely it would be for her mom to be here. "Nope, just me. My god, you got so tall. I haven't seen you since ninth grade."

"You look almost exactly the same Jadey. Except, well ... heck, you're taller too." He laughed nervously. "But just as cute," he added. Jadey smiled and whispered a shy "thank you."

She looked around the house at her grandma's furniture, which had gathered a little dust since her passing.

"I'm sorry I don't have any refreshments or anything. I just got here about an hour ago and haven't even walked through the whole place yet. I haven't dared open the refrigerator."

"That's okay, I can't stay. I'm working the second shift and have to be at work soon. My brother and I opened a car repair shop about four years ago and it takes both of us to keep it up and running."

"You're in business with Ray? I didn't think you two even got along. Of course, he was two years older and hated to hang around with his younger brother."

"He's still two years older, coincidentally." They both smiled at his joke. "But we get along pretty good. He ended up marrying Judy Lee, you know."

"No, I didn't know. My grandma didn't really pass on much news from town when we got together. Who did you marry, Doug?"

"No ring on my finger. I sometimes see a girl over in Oakdale, but her two kids are little sh... um, brats, and I don't see myself hitching that wagon, you know?"

"I get it." Jadey found herself wondering what to say. What to ask about. How weird seeing a boy she had had a crush on in ninth grade, now grown to be a man. He wasn't exactly the way she remembered because he had been kind of gangly and shy. She could still sense a bit of that shyness in him now, but he had grown into quite a handsome man. The silence grew longer.

"Well, I gotta go, but I wanted to just say hi, and, um, welcome back, and, I don't know, let's get together with some of the old gang soon. A lot of them still live in the area. You know Katie's still here."

"Katie Holman?"

"The Jadey and Katie Show. That's what you two always called yourselves."

Jadey laughed at the memory. "Katie Holman. I'm looking forward to seeing her again. Maybe we can all meet up for dinner in the next couple of days? Let me get my bearings here first."

Doug smiled and nodded. He looked back at the door, as if reluctant to go. "See you soon, Jadey. It sure is good to have you back."

Jadey watched him walk down her front step and head for his pickup truck. Boy, this was going to be interesting.

Chapter 3

Sergeant Greg Dillanian left the Gerald County, Wisconsin courtroom and nearly ran into his boss, Police Chief Howard Dent. The older man carried his extra 40 pounds around his waist and a superiority complex in his head. Dent had always been an "old-school cop," with the uniform shirt buttoned to the top and a navy-blue tie dangling in front. "Crisp but stuffed" came to Dillanian's mind every time he saw the chief, whose clothes were stretched to their maximum thread count. Dent's face was leathery from decades of being outside in every kind of weather. His complexion was what people used to call "swarthy," back when people talked like that.

"Dillanian. How'd it go?"

"Not the first time I've testified in an assault trial, but probably the messiest. When the accused is the brother-in-law of the victim, let's just say the family dynamics are wonky."

"Wonky. They teach you how to talk like a teenager in that fancy eastern school, Sergeant?"

Dillanian shrugged and forced a smile. This was an ongoing verbal icepick from a guy who inserted the word "eastern" into any conversation as a means of ham-handedly setting anyone below his rank in their place. Dillanian had spent one year at a small college in New Hampshire, but then graduated from the University of Missouri.

The two turned and walked out of the court house.

"So, I heard Ellie Evans' granddaughter came back in town. Any idea what her plans are?"

"Not really," Dillanian answered. "Her car was loaded with stuff like she was here to stay for a bit, and I saw some tools on the floor of the back seat. The back end was sitting low so the trunk was full too."

Dent frowned.

"I might have to stop in and welcome her. See what she might be up to."

Dillanian stole a quick side glance at his boss.

"Appeared to be back to see what she inherited," Dillanian offered. "When the papers were filed showing her as the heir, you figured she'd show up eventually, right?"

"Sure. I just want to know how long she plans on hanging around."

Chapter 4

Jadey's fourth day in the house started the same as days two and three. She pulled herself out of the narrow twin bed she slept in as a child and took a minute to look around the room. She still felt both odd and comforted to note how little her grandma changed it since the last time she slept here before she and her mom went running. She bent over to stretch her muscles, and for the third morning in a row thought about how her old bed was not quite as comfortable as she remembered. But she couldn't imagine sleeping in either her mother's or grandma's bed.

Her dresser still had the nicks from where she tried to carve her name with the jackknife her grandma gave her for her tenth birthday. Yesterday, she finally placed her grown-up socks and underwear in the same drawers where she used to stuff her childhood clothes, and the ridiculously small closet held a few of her shirts and sun-dresses. She stacked jeans and shorts in tilting piles on the floor until she figured out a better system.

Before heading downstairs to make coffee, she once again wandered into her grandma's bedroom. Jadey's mom had the bedroom at the south end of the upstairs at the end of a long dark hallway. Her grandma's bedroom at the top of the stairs enjoyed light from two large windows, which made it bright and cheerful. Unlike Jadey's bedroom, her grandma's had a large closet, and Jadey knew that she'd soon have to undertake the task of going through her grandma's things and donating or throwing away as necessary. It could wait, though. Her first task was to finish the demo job on the kitchen.

She turned to go back downstairs but paused for a moment to look more closely at a small photo in a frame on the dresser. Jadey and her grandma had posed in front of a giraffe habitat at a zoo, one of her favorite trips during happier times. In the background, a giraffe reached for leaves on a high branch of a tree, and in the foreground stood the two family members who did not resemble each other in many ways. Her grandmother, like her own mother, was of Scandinavian descent and had the milky white skin and blonde hair to prove it. Her own look was a bit more exotic, with a more mocha-colored skin and dark, curly hair. Jadey had never met her father and, having been born in 1991, she understood the times made it tough for this small town to leave their prejudices behind and accept a relationship between a Black man and a White woman. But did he know about her? Did he ever try to meet her? Attempts to dig into answers in the past had always been met with deflection from her mother.

She set the photo back on the dresser and headed down the stairs.

Jadey's trunkful of tools were getting good use. Early in life, she discovered an ability to fix almost anything, mostly out of necessity. Her mom's response to broken hinges and peeling caulk would be to get overwhelmed, complain about the long list of things that weren't working, and then kind of shut down and do nothing. Grandma had been a bit handier because her own father let her hang out with him in his workshop. But overall, the two adult women seemed satisfied to let things go as long as possible. A young Jadey took that as a challenge.

After the first walk-through of her grandma's house three days before, she knew everything else could wait until she did something about the kitchen. She remembered the house had been built in 1945, and although quite sturdy, no one was going to get excited about the old appliances, even the ones that still worked. And there was absolutely no hope of ever getting the inside of the aging oven clean again.

The refrigerator, which had taken her an entire day to empty and scrub out, made panting sounds, like a dog left out in the sun. There wasn't a dishwasher, nor was there room for one in the current configuration, and pretty much none of the drawers opened without exerting superhuman muscle power.

Definitely a complete demo job, which she started on day two.

This morning, coffee cup in hand, she eyed the wall separating the half torn-up kitchen from the dining room. Without bothering with her normal internal debate, she made an instant decision to take it down. The house would have to do without a formal dining room going forward because she had a vision of an expanded kitchen with a corner dinette. Maybe some teal colors. A little magenta for accents. A sliding door to the backyard to replace the aging windows. Her mind flashed with dozens of different ideas and she found herself getting excited.

This was going to be a total kitchen makeover, and she had the time and the money to do it. The previous year had been a whirlwind of book signing events across six different states, and a series of appearances on various local television cable shows promoting her novel. The climb into the bestseller list still astounded her, but she thought back on the three years of writing late into the night after work, and giving up weekends and vacations. She periodically reminded herself she had earned every bit of that word "bestseller."

But the devil on her other shoulder continued to whisper in her ear that if she didn't write another bestseller follow-up, she would just be a one-hit-wonder fraud. It kept her both motivated and terrified. The move back to Twin Station and an enticing remodeling job ahead of her was the perfect distraction.

With a toolbelt wrapped around the waistband of her cut-off jeans, she silently prayed to the remodeling gods no plumbing or heating pipes ran between the studs. Her eyes spotted the small area grandma had roughly patched with spackle so many years ago. Wincing, she remembered the moment her mom had paused in the middle of an argument and picked up a frying pan. Like a discus thrower from a scene out of Athens, her mother had hurled the pan at the wall, leaving behind a dent, and Grandma in tears.

That was the spot where Jadey took the first swing of her sledgehammer.

Three hours later, Jadey stared at the piles of broken drywall at her feet, her beat-up work boots covered with drywall dust. The aging air conditioner in the house had given a valiant effort, but couldn't put much of a dent in the hot air outside as the midday sun beat down on the house. Her hair was sticky, and sawdust clung to every part of her skin, making it hard to even use the back of her hand to wipe sweat from her face.

Picking up a stack of drywall pieces, she pushed open the back door to where the Twin Station Public Works Department left the rented dumpster. Lost in thought about the work she had ahead of her, she jumped when she noticed a man standing ten feet from her. His stare was familiar.

Chapter 5

Jadey recognized Sgt. Dillanian, the officer who had shared a gallon of gas from his squad car to help her limp into town four days before. She felt unnerved by his sudden appearance, while at the same time couldn't help but admit he looked absolutely fantastic standing there in her grandma's backyard, the sun shining on his face. Oh god, what a face!

"Still not a serial killer," she blurted out after a lengthy stare-down between the two.

"I think we've pretty well cleared you on suspicion of mass murder," he finally offered. He crossed the space between them and looked into the dumpster.

"Complete demo?"

Jadey heaved the stack of drywall over the sides of the dumpster and then wiped her chalky palms on the sides of her shorts.

"I'm not sure yet. I'm tackling the kitchen and dining room first and then I'll see what's left of my savings account and work ethic."

"Thinking of resale, or are you here to stay?"

"Boy, you just cut right to the point, don't you? No small talk, like 'Have you found any signs of mice or vagrants yet?'"

"I'm going to guess mice wouldn't faze you, and if there were any vagrants hiding in your walls you would have put them to work."

"Probably right. If they're going to live here, they're going to have to knock down a wall or two."

Dillanian looked up toward the second floor of the house, and then back to the dumpster. "You're going to need a bigger dumpster before you get done."

"Hey, I'm the mastermind who couldn't even make sure she had enough gas in the tank for an eighty-mile drive, so the chances of me miscalculating how big a dumpster I'm going to need are pretty good. Come on in. At least I have some lemonade made."

Dillanian followed her in through the back door and whistled when he saw the work she had done and the mess on the floor.

"You did all this in just two days? By yourself?"

"And I didn't even cut through any electrical wires or accidentally dislodge a load-bearing beam. I'm considering it a total win."

He accepted the glass of lemonade she poured, noting the refrigerator was sparkling clean on the inside but only held a pitcher of lemonade and the remains of a pizza.

"So how does someone who knows their way around a ten-pound sledgehammer and the demo of a framing wall forget to fill the gas tank?"

Jadey laughed and sipped her lemonade. How much should she reveal about herself to an almost stranger?

"My ex-boyfriend used to accuse me of intentionally sabotaging things so I wouldn't have to actually confront a problem. Like tough jobs. Relationship issues. Little stuff like that. I apparently used to purposely start arguments whenever he brought up long-term plans."

Her comment was met by the now-familiar stare from Dillanian.

"So, you were avoiding a long-term relationship with your gas tank?"

She shrugged. "Maybe I was subconsciously hesitant about actually coming back to Twin Station."

She paused.

"Or is that too woo-woo for you?"

"Not sure about woo-woo, but it sounds like you took some psychology classes in college. I'm going to guess an English major with a Psych minor."

Jadey paused, her lemonade glass halfway to her lips. "You looked me up. I'm not sure if I should be flattered or terrified."

"I'm a cop. I look people up."

She looked at him quietly and a minute of silence passed between them.

"No beer?"

"Huh?"

He pointed to the refrigerator. "I noticed the pizza, but no beer. Doesn't everybody drink beer with pizza?"

She grinned, relaxing a bit at his feeble attempt at humor. "I bought a six-pack the day I drove into town, three days ago. It's been gone for two days."

The corner of Dillanian's mouth showed a hint of a grin.

"Oh, you do smile. Is it possible you possess the human genetic code for mirth?"

"Mirth? Do people talk like that?"

"Deflection. And yes, I talk like that. Are you capable of humor?"

"Capable? Possibly. But not likely. I smile when I have a beer with my pizza but it's probably just an autonomic response."

"Autonomic. Do people talk like that?"

"Touché."

Jadey stacked some more drywall pieces to keep herself busy. Dillanian unnerved her, but she couldn't put her finger on why. Why did he show up here? What's with the horror movie silent creep-up-behind-her thing? She tried for small talk.

"I don't remember you being here when I was a kid. I think I would have remembered you, or at least the name Dillanian. Please don't tell me I'm older than you."

"I wasn't here then. I transferred here less than a year ago from a police department in Missouri."

"How did you end up in a small town in Wisconsin? Do you have family close by?"

"Nope. Just saw an opportunity. What are you going to do with all of these old appliances?"

Nifty change of subject, Jadey noticed.

"None of them is worth crap. I checked and there's a salvage place in Oakdale that will take them. I assume they strip out anything useful before junking them. One of my old school friends offered his truck to haul them for me."

"Doug Baylor?"

Jadey jerked to attention. "You know a lot. Why do I get the feeling you're not just here for a casual visit?"

"I know Doug and Ray because they've fixed my car. It's a small town." Dillanian wandered around the room, looking at the exposed stud walls and dusty hardwood floors.

"And getting smaller every minute. If there is anything else you want to know about me, how about you come and ask me instead of creeping around behind my back?"

The last words came out a little harsher than she intended. Silence filled the space until Dillanian tipped his head to her.

"You got it. Good luck with the rest of the demo work."

He stepped back out the door and disappeared around the corner of the house.

Jadey wrapped her arms around herself, feeling a familiar barrier going up.

Chapter 6

Downtown hadn't changed much in the years Jadey had been gone. Most of the storefronts looked the same, although she saw the dentist's office had expanded into the space next to it, which meant Mason's Grocery Store was gone. Maybe they moved to another end of town, she hoped. At least four more restaurants had appeared, and they looked pretty interesting compared to the old diners and Dairy Queen that used to be the only options.

She found the shop at the end of Coral Street and pulled in front. The sign in the window made her laugh. "Katie's Kuts." Yep, good old Katie, she thought. Goofiest kid in school, but my best friend and confidant. Well, she corrected herself. Not exactly true on the confidant part. Jadey hadn't shared a lot of things with anyone. Not even Katie.

She stared at the sign for a minute, and then ventured inside.

Two women sitting in chairs chatted amiably with each other, while stylists did interesting things to their hair. Jadey didn't recognize either of the women behind the chairs, and she suddenly had a thought that maybe after all these years she wouldn't know what Katie even looked like anymore. Could one of those women be Katie?

Her confusion was broken a minute later when another woman came into the room from a back office and Jadey almost laughed aloud. Oh my gosh, Katie really hadn't changed one bit. The same blonde curls, the dimpled cheeks, and extra-sized bosoms which used to kind of intrigue Jadey when they were fourteen. Yes, this was Katie.

Katie's eyes lit up when she saw Jadey and she almost ran to give her a hug.

"You made it! I can't believe you're here. When you called, I thought it was like a voice from the past."

"I guess it kind of was. And you. Good grief! You look exactly the same. Have you aged at all since ninth grade?"

Katie struck a model pose and smiled. "Hey girl, we're not even thirty yet. Not too many miles on this treasure, you know? By the way, I love the auburn streaks in your hair. Nice touch."

"Yep, you're still the same Katie. It's all about the hair." They both laughed.

Jadey fingered her hair self-consciously.

"I just did this last night, from a box. Sorry."

"No worries. I'll get you in one of those chairs eventually and we'll really doll you up. Come on in back. We have to catch up."

Jadey followed Katie to the back room where she instantly recognized Katie's style in the décor of the small office. Pink and mint green curtains on the window. Stacks of books everywhere, filled with color pictures of hair styles. A desk painted turquoise with a chair that would fit in well at Buckingham Palace. That was Katie. Eclectic. Exciting. Cute. Not afraid to set her own trends.

"I can't believe you actually did it. You always said you wanted to own a hair salon, and you even picked out the name 'Katie's Kuts' back in fifth grade. Way to go!"

Katie smiled with pride. "And how about you? A bestselling author? Finally, all of that scribbling in your notebook paid off big time. And constantly reading. You always had a book in your hands and I used to call you 'Eyeballs' because all I could ever see were your eyes. Everything else was buried in a book."

"We were kind of weird, weren't we?" Jadey laughed.

"The last two customers will be done soon, and then we close up. I keep some wine in the mini-fridge here, so we can finally crack open a bottle and be legal."

"Oh my god! I had forgotten the time when we snuck a bottle of wine from your parents' liquor cabinet and ran into the woods with it. It took us forever to get the cork out of it, and then we realized we didn't have any glasses."

"I remember you saying 'Katie, we're not legal and we're not that smart.' But we definitely drank enough to get sick."

"We thought we were so cool. Until we started throwing up. I wanted to lay down right there in the woods and go to sleep, but you were the one with common sense and made me go home. I even wrote a story later that I called 'Kommon Sense Katie.'"

Katie pulled a bottle from the mini-fridge and started to work the corkscrew. "I don't know about any common sense, but I do know I've got better taste in wine than my parents."

Chapter 7

Jadey sipped on her glass of wine while Katie went out to the front to see the last customers and her two stylists out the door. Locked up, with the CLOSED sign turned in the window, she rejoined Jadey in the back room.

"What do you know about this Sgt. Dillanian, the cop?" Jadey asked Katie, who was pouring a fresh glass for herself.

"Oh my, oh my. Only back in town for a week and you've already got your hooks on the best eye candy in town. You do have good taste, girlfriend." Katie smiled conspiratorially.

"No, no, it's not that. It's just, I don't know. I only saw him the one time when I ran out of gas coming into town, and then all of a sudden, he showed up at my grandma's house. I wasn't sure if I should be creeped out or something."

"Oh, to be creeped out by a gorgeous thing like him. He took the job back in about November? Maybe October? Half the women in town have been making excuses to call the police. Cat in a tree. Neighbor borrowed my hose and hasn't returned it.... Even I have made up reasons to walk past the police station, in my best high heels, of course, just looking for a chance to make conversation."

Jadey laughed and held up her hand to stop her friend. "Okay, yeah, he's pretty good looking. I mean if you like a long, lean body type, with an amazing face on top."

She paused, enjoying the memory. "But have you ever actually seen him smile? Does he have anything remotely like a personality?"

"I'll take personality from my yappy customers and settle for 'long, lean body type' in my bed." Katie took a sip of wine. "I'd tell you good luck, but so far I haven't seen him give a woman a second glance the whole time he's been here. Maybe he's gay."

"That would be fine with me," Jadey spoke from her glass. "My two best friends back home are gay, and they're more fun to be around than half the guys I've dated."

"Really? You hang around with gay guys? I mean I know it's not contagious, but do you have to go to a second mass to dip your fingers in holy water afterward?"

Jadey looked up, uncomfortable, trying to determine if Katie might be joking. But her friend was already on to another topic.

"Doug wants to get all of us together for a dinner out this weekend. Catch up on old times. Hang out with a superstar."

Jadey snorted a little wine through her nose and started coughing. Katie handed her a tissue and laughed.

"Hey, you're the only famous person who ever left this town, Jade. I saw an article about one of your book signings in Minneapolis. I wanted to go but I had to run the shop."

"You'd be amazed at how UNfamous a first-time author is. I practically had to perform acrobatic feats of daring just to get people to come in the door to take a look at my book. It's only a good seller because I lucked onto an amazing agent who is kind of new to the field. She only has five authors under her wings so she works 18-hour days to sell me. I just got lucky. If I write a second big seller, then I'll start to believe."

"But I read the book. *Westmore Wombats*. I had no idea how funny you are. Any of those quirky characters based on any of us?"

"Not consciously. I seem to have been blessed with a really weird imagination, or as I like to call it, 'a bottomless pit of stupid stuff in my head.'"

Katie laughed.

"Let's definitely do dinner though. I kind of kept up on some town news through my grandma over the years, but I want to hear it from you and Doug and the rest."

"Maybe you and Doug can pick up where you left off in ninth grade. You two sure had google-eyes for each other."

They both laughed at the memory. "Google-eyes. I haven't heard that expression in years. I had such a crush on him since about fifth grade and used to imagine that we'd end up married."

"And then you had to go and move out of town and break his heart."

Jadey's smile faded. "Well, things don't usually work out the way you picture it when you're a kid. I'm looking forward to seeing what everyone grew into."

"He found someone to fix that broken heart, Jadey. At least for a while. Two months after we graduated from high school, Doug and I got married."

Jadey stared at Katie, waiting for the punchline. "What? I mean, are you serious? You two are married?" Her heart pounded in her chest. Doug married to Katie?

"Well, not anymore, of course." Katie was nonchalant with the retelling. She stared up at the ceiling, wine glass in one hand, fingers playing with her curls with the other.

"It was one of those, I don't know, marriages of convenience, I guess? We had just graduated. Neither of us had a clue what we were going to do next. All of a sudden we had this little fling and just decided to get married."

Katie shrugged, pretending none of it mattered.

"I was the dumb one. I thought I was marrying the cutest guy in school, but between the fact he had never gotten over you, and also had a secret love child, it was doomed from the start."

"Wait. What? He had a child? You're going to have to start from the beginning, Katie girl."

Katie smiled, knowing she had Jadey's full attention.

"So, you're going to completely skip the part about him never having gotten over you?"

"We'll get back to that later. Spill!"

"It seems Doug got a little too randy in our junior year with a first cousin that lived on a farm outside of town. It was all totally top secret. The funny thing is, later, when Doug and I were married, I met that cousin, and I liked her. And she had the cutest little girl named Mindy. Once in a while Doug and I would even babysit Mindy when Kim had a date, or just needed a break, and all the while it turned out the kid was Doug's. I guess most of the family knew, but it was one of those things no one talked about."

Jadey just stared at Katie for a second, stunned by the story.

"And he just let you babysit his own daughter, without ever telling you? Wasn't he doing some kind of co-parenting or something? Was he sending child support payments?

"Good questions, and all part of the many reasons he and I didn't last. He and Kim agreed she would be the full-time single mom because I guess they both admitted he'd be a terrible dad. He did send small payments every month, which I only found out about at the end because he had a secret bank account for her, but she and the baby lived with her folks and I guess everyone there pitched in."

"Bizarre. And sad. So, you and Doug divorced, but seemed to have stayed friends."

"It's true. We're much better suited to be friends than married. So, of course that means he's available if your heart is still pounding for him like it was in ninth grade."

"I've got a lot to digest. He was definitely my crush, and he's still adorable. And from what I've seen so far, he seems like a great guy. But I didn't come here looking for a husband, so...."

Katie laughed. "You've barely been here a week. Let's give this all some time. And, of course, there's the eye candy over at Twin Station PD."

The two continued talking for another half hour, but Jadey eventually let out a sigh.

"We might have to block out an entire weekend to fully catch up. Bring inner tubes over to the lake? Slather on some sunscreen?"

"Sounds good to me, but keep in mind I work weekend days."

Katie put the glasses in a small sink in her office and grabbed her own purse and sunglasses. They walked out the front door where Katie locked up again.

"What was the deal with you and your mom leaving town so fast anyway? And never even coming back for visits? You were only across the border and, like, seventy miles away."

Jadey sighed. "Boy, it's a really long story, which I'll save for another time. My mom and grandma had been on a continuous 'falling out' path for years, and things finally came to a head, I guess. Even though mom wouldn't really talk to her own mom, or come back here, my grandma and I stayed in touch and once a year she'd come pick me up in Minneapolis and the two of us would take a trip together. Never anything fancy – Mt. Rushmore, or Door County. The best week we spent was when we stayed at a motel in the Twin Cities. She bet me we could swim in a different lake every day of the week, which we did, and then spent our evenings at the Mall of America on the rides. She was so cool."

"I really liked her, and was sad when she died. Fell down the stairs I heard."

"It still seems so strange. She was so healthy. I can't imagine her losing her balance, although about a month ago I fell off a curb and twisted my ankle, so anything's possible. My grandma's journals were in her bedroom, all lined up in order, and I've been having some fun reading and going down memory lane, but there's nothing more recent than a couple of years ago. I'm trying to find the recent ones to see if she wrote anything about some health issues."

"Your grandma kept journals?"

"All the time. She got me started on journaling too, when I was about eight. It's why you always saw me writing stories in a notebook, and was probably the biggest single habit that got me where I am today."

Neither spoke for a moment, until Katie broke the silence. "We have so much more catching up to do. I'll see you on Saturday when we do dinner with the gang. Maybe the start-up of your unfinished love story with Doug."

The two hugged and separated at their cars.

"The Jadey and Katie Show is on again," yelled Katie as she backed out of her parking space.

Jadey sat in her car for an extra minute. This was like old times, but in a bit of a surreal way. It was almost like watching an old movie, but in this case, with a tiny element of darkness in it, a harbinger of things to come. She had a lot of tough decisions ahead of her, and there was something she couldn't put her finger on that didn't feel quite right.

Chapter 8

Saturday began with Jadey again in her work clothes, using a small crowbar to pry the remaining trim from the walls and door jambs in the kitchen. She looked around at all of the areas where drywall nails protruded from the studs, and spoke to the crowbar, promising it would get a workout today. The work was dusty, dirty, and muscle-aching, but Jadey loved it. She also had her mind on the dinner planned for that evening with Katie, Doug and two other friends from her time of living in Twin Station. She had met "Jeanie B." as everyone called her, in seventh grade when the Buckmans moved to Twin Station from Madison. Jadey recognized a little of herself in Jeanie, who was friendly, but shy about starting all new friendships in a new school. Their seventh-grade social studies teacher paired the two of them for a project on Susan B. Anthony, and the bond held until Jadey moved away two years later.

A classmate named Chad would be there too. He and Doug lived next door to each other in those days. The two of them played sports together and were pretty much inseparable, so the crush Jadey had on Doug meant she saw a lot of Chad too. Chad's dad died of something which caused his heart to suddenly stop, so Chad was the only other person Jadey knew in school who didn't have a dad at home. There seemed to be a bit of a shared alliance between Jadey and Chad, although being teenagers, it was entirely unspoken.

The day flew by, and at about 3:00 Jadey realized she hadn't stopped for lunch. She grabbed an apple and washed it in the bathroom sink, which was where everything had to be washed right now. Was she crazy to tear apart the kitchen without a real plan in place? How long would it take before she could actually cook and do her own dishes in the bare, empty space she looked at now?

Two hours later, she jumped in the shower and let the hot water run over her sore muscles. She lost track of time, her mind darting between plans for the kitchen and the evening ahead of her. Eventually, the shower water started to get cold, and she knew she had daydreamed too long. Grabbing her towel, she rubbed herself dry and pulled on one of her favorite sundresses. The pastel periwinkle and cream colors were a perfect complement for her soft skin that her ex-boyfriend used to say reminded him of toffee.

She fussed with her hair a bit, slid her feet into some sandals, and then stared into the mirror. She reached into her cosmetic bag and pulled out the false eyelashes she had bought on a lark the previous year. *I'm so not a false eyelash girl,* she thought to herself, but she applied them anyway and blinked at her reflection. *Let's see if my eyelids are exhausted by the end of the night.* Smiling, she headed down the stairs and out the door.

When she walked into The Bag O' Bones, one of Twin Station's newer restaurants, Katie and Doug were already sitting at the table, and for a second Jadey was struck by the knowledge those two friends had once been married, and shared a bed together. How strange the way things can flip so much in a world where you thought you knew exactly how everything was supposed to go. The two smiled when they saw her and pointed to the chair between them. Within a few moments both Chad and Jeanie had arrived, and everyone shared hugs, happy for the chance for a reunion.

The Bag O' Bones was not really named for what it looked like. In a nod to the style favored by Gen X'ers and Millennials, the owners had chosen a minimalist grunge style. The building had previously housed a two-story car parts store, so the new owners removed the first-floor ceiling and made great use out of exposed ductwork, creating an intentional "refurbished factory" look. Blonde wood countertops had been buffed to a high shine. Exposed brick walls provided hanging places for metal sculptures and retro-neon signs. Servers passed out bendable silver menus mimicking the look of sheets of aluminum.

The talk was light and fun. The food was delicious. They each took turns bringing Jadey up to date on what they had been doing for the past dozen years, and Jadey shared a little about her life since moving to the Twin Cities. How interesting to see how quickly they fell into such familiarity, as if the years hadn't separated them at all. Jeanie, married and raising a four-year-old boy, declared proudly she was expecting baby number two. Chad started his family even earlier and showed pictures of his wife and the eight-year-old twins on a farm just outside of town.

About an hour into the dinner, when the group leaned back in their chairs and switched to after-dinner drinks, the talk turned to some quieter topics. Jeanie was the one to broach the question everyone at the table wanted to ask.

"How come you never came back to Twin Station, Jadey? I mean to visit. I understand from what you've told us why your mom might not have wanted to come and stay at your grandma's house, but heck, you were only a couple of hours away. Once you got your driver's license, how come we never saw you?"

Jadey saw everyone lean in, waiting for her response. She took another drink of beer to stall for a minute.

"It's kind of hard to explain. Even though I had a great relationship with my grandma, I think some of my mom's anxiety about the town and the house probably ended up absorbed into my subconscious. I knew my mom and her mom had, oh gosh, I guess tons of issues. But for my mom it was more than that and I guess ... it's hard to explain because I never thought about it consciously, but I suppose I felt it would have been disloyal to her to come back, when this was the source of so much sadness for her."

Jeanie shrugged. "Makes sense. Even when we're real snots to our parents, we don't want to actually do something to hurt them. At least not a big hurt like that. I'm just glad you came back now."

The conversation turned to more reminiscing about school days when Jadey noticed movement at the front door of the restaurant and saw a big man walk in. He was out of uniform, but she recognized him as the chief of police because his face was on posters in shop windows all over town. "Thanks For Visiting Twin Station, and Come Again Soon." Corny slogan, but small towns needed a boost in tourism. The incongruity of seeing him in civilian clothes at first startled her, and reminded her he wasn't just the Chief of Police. He lived in town too, and probably went to the barber shop and the grocery store like everyone else.

She watched as his eyes scanned the tables, his movements quiet. He reminded her of a wolf, searching the woods for prey. She didn't realize she was so focused on watching him until his eyes met hers and she quickly looked away, trying to pretend she was just looking at a picture on the wall. She tuned back into the conversation at the table but then noticed Katie had turned to look at Dent too. Jadey couldn't read into the look on Katie's face, but there seemed to be a slight change in the way Katie sat in the chair, and when Katie's focus returned to the people at the table, she appeared to be distracted, almost jittery.

Chapter 9

Ten busy days in Twin Station and Jadey could see some progress on the remodel at her grandma's house. She found she couldn't quite get herself to call it *her* house, even though her grandma chose her to inherit it. It would always be grandma's house in her heart, and she still hadn't made any kind of decision about her long-term plans there. Back in The Twin Cities, her apartment was subleased to a good friend, but the agree-ment was only for a year, which gave her time to figure out what her future would look like.

She looked around the empty space where the kitchen and dining room used to be. Everything was gone now, including the refrigerator. She bought herself a mini-fridge to keep a few things cold, but put the old, dying refrigerator on the same truck that took the other applian-ces to the salvage yard. Newly delivered drywall filled one corner where the dining room used to be. Jadey shuddered when she thought about installing those large pieces alone. She looked at the old insulation that hung between the studs and sighed, remembering she planned to replace it before nailing up the new drywall.

In the meantime, old newspapers became cut-out templates of cabinets and appliances, and Jadey had been moving them around every day, trying to determine the best layout for the new space. This morning she simply rubbed her eyes and spoke to the bare walls.

"Dammit. Every version I try looks super for the first five minutes, but then stupid after that. I should have gone to kitchen-design school!"

Her eyes strayed to the stairway leading upstairs, and she soon found herself climbing up, looking straight ahead into her grandma's bedroom. Since she had been back, she wandered into the space at least once a day, touching the sweater her grandma left draped across the back of her rocker, giving a little puff of her grandma's perfume so she could maintain the dream of her grandma just walking back through the front door again. She hadn't yet brought herself to really go through her grandma's belongings, but maybe today. Maybe it was time to sort through some things and see what could go to the charity drive at the church.

But not the pictures. Jadey would never part with the pictures. All over the room, photos reminded her of happier times. The memories of yearly vacations they shared made her both smile and tear up. Each year they wore different, silly hats, and those were the pictures that made her laugh the most.

Not for the first time Jadey wondered how such a loving grandma could have had such a fallout with her only child. And even though Jadey knew some hidden history in this town left her mom with scars, how had she not found the comfort she needed with her own mom?

A picture of herself in a pretty silver frame caught her eye, and she remembered seeing the same frame on a different picture, many years ago.

•••••

Ten-year old Jadey, looking through a box of her grandma's keepsakes, found her grandparents' wedding picture, upside down at the very bottom of the dusty box. She ran her fingers around the beautiful frame and called out to her grandma to come and see.

When Ellie Evans came into the room, Jadey held up the picture. "Is this you and grandpa? I've never seen a picture of him before."

Her grandma's face fell, and she slowly walked toward her granddaughter, taking the picture from her hands. "Yes, this is your grandpa, on our wedding day."

"You don't look very happy in the picture, Grandma." The smile on the young bride's face looked forced, like a hostage pretending for her abductor everything was fine.

"And Grandpa looks almost mad. Was he angry about something?"

Grandma Ellie paused. "Honestly Jadey, your grandpa was pretty much always mad."

"About what?"

"The birds chirping. Morning sun. His eggs over-cooked. It didn't take much to make that man mad."

"What happened to Grandpa? Where did he go?"

"We're not sure, sweetheart. But it's pretty much okay just that he went. One day he was here and the next day he wasn't, and that was the day I started packing up his stuff. I thought I'd gotten rid of this old picture."

Ellie opened the back of the frame and pulled the picture out, crumpling it in her hands. "This is a nice frame. I think I'll put a picture of you in it now."

•••••

Jadey put down the frame and thought about the memory. Grandma had been so matter-of-fact about the way her husband had just left. So many secrets. She wished she could ask a thousand questions. Looking at her grandma's closet door, she held her breath a little as she opened it, and then smiled at what she saw. A row of simple, practical blouses hung on the rod, along with two efficient dresses for the occasional funeral or special occasion Ellie attended. The boxes on the shelf were probably stuffed with those silly hats. Was she ready to look at those yet? Although a little dust had built up on the floor under the hanging clothes, Jadey recognized her grandma's orderly nature. A laundry basket had just a few things waiting to be washed. Six pairs of shoes, all comfortable and practical lined the floor. An array of hooks on the back of the door held a couple of belts and scarves.

She remembered her younger days when her grandma's closet was a perfect hiding place for her to curl up with a book. The exposed bulb in the ceiling had a long string she could reach even when she was quite young, so she'd open the door, pull the string, and then hide herself in the back corner and get lost in other worlds.

Something nagged at her now, and she parted the hanging blouses to look at the back wall of the closet. It's so funny how things seem so much bigger when you're a kid. This closet was enormous, wasn't it?

Her view of the back wall through the parted blouses confused her. The wall was the same color as the rest of the closet, but instead of drywall, it looked like it was made of wood, instead. She didn't remember that, but then it's not something she would have noticed as a kid. And clearly her grandma had repainted the entire closet because she was sure it used to be kind of a tan color, but now was a more modern mauve.

She straightened up the blouses and was about to leave the closet when something made her turn back for another look. This time she slid aside the blouses at the end of the rod and could see that where the painted wood met up in the corner with the drywall, a small hook protruded. Curious, she put her finger into the bend of the hook and pulled. Nothing happened, but then why should it? Maybe a belt or something had once hung there. Still feeling like something wasn't quite right, she tried turning the hook and found, with a little effort, she could turn it a quarter of the way to the left. Once she did, she heard a quiet click. The wall moved a bit, and now, with a push, it gave way. Hidden hinges allowed the wall to swing in, like a door.

With a little effort she was able to squeeze in past the opening and peer behind the makeshift door. Here was the rest of the favorite spot she remembered from her childhood. Her grandma built herself a safe-room, hidden in the back of her closet.

Chapter 10

Jadey looked around the small space, knowing what she was seeing, but not really believing. In the roughly six-foot by four-foot room, created by walling off half of her grandma's large closet, the floor held a beat-up couch cushion, two flashlights with extra batteries stacked next to them, and a small box full of wrapped crackers, a jar of peanut butter, and some chocolates. On the other end of the room was a plastic bucket, empty but stained with something Jadey didn't want to know about.

The realization this was a safe-room, prepared for someone to stay for a long stretch of time, sent a shudder through Jadey's body, weakening her knees with a combination of fear and confusion.

What could possibly have frightened her grandma so much she painstakingly cleared out half her closet, built a wall in it, and furnished it with some kind of comforts to allow her to stay for hours or more at a time? It was then what the bucket was for hit her, and seeing a roll of toilet paper in the box of foodstuffs confirmed her thought.

She barely had a chance to process the secret room when the sound of her doorbell ringing made her jump.

For just a second, her instinct was to hide. To close the door of the secret room with her inside and pretend she wasn't there. But what was she afraid of? Whatever it was that so frightened her grandma had nothing to do with her, right?

Her face felt flushed with a mixture of awe and confusion and urgency. She carefully closed the secret door, turning the hook to make sure it latched properly, and then rearranged the clothes on the rod back to their places of hiding the door. By the time she reached the top of the stairs to head down, the doorbell rang again.

She could see Doug's face in the small window in the door, so she allowed herself to relax as she reached it and turn the knob.

"Hi, Doug. Sorry it took me a minute. I was, um ... in the bathroom."

"No problem. Sorry if I caught you at a bad time. I wanted to see the progress you've made on the house."

Jadey flashed back to the conversation they'd had a couple of nights before, when the old high school friends had gotten together for dinner. Jadey described the work she had done to demo the kitchen and dining room and had them all laughing with her description of pulling down a chunk of drywall and having ancient drywall dust puff up in a cloud and end up in her bra. Doug had seen a part of her work because he helped her haul away the appliances, but he was curious to see what it looked like now.

As she guided Doug back into what used to be the kitchen, Jadey found herself glancing back up the stairs, her mind on the safe-room. Trying to steer her thoughts back to the present, she joked about the chaos she created.

"I swept up the last of the mess and started to lay out some kind of templates of where I might place the new cabinets and sink and appliances. It looks like I'll have room for a pretty good-sized island too, which to me is the most exciting part."

Jadey caught Doug looking her way, smiling at her enthusiasm.

"It looks like you might be planning to stay," Doug said quietly. "What with all the plans you're making."

Jadey hesitated. "Probably. Maybe. I'm still not exactly sure what my plans are. I figure whether I stay or decide to sell, the kitchen needed a complete makeover for whoever lives here. But this is the first time I've been able to actually design something the way I want it to be, so I'm having some fun."

"Do you know about things like plumbing and electricity, and codes and stuff?" Doug looked at her skeptically.

"Actually, I do, believe it or not. I've been fixing and repairing lots of things around the house since I was a kid. But I have someone coming over from Oakdale next week to do all of my measurements for cabinets and countertops, and give me some advice. This is too big to do all on my own."

"If you need help installing the cabinets when they come, I'm pretty good at lifting and holding a level. I'm mostly good at working on cars, but I'd be glad to help with whatever."

"That's nice. Thanks, Doug. Remember the time we worked on the ninth-grade dance party? You and I built a fake waterfall out of barnwood and Styrofoam. We used the wrong kind of glue, nails that were too short to hold the wood pieces together, and then banged it against a few walls just carrying it into the gym. The crazy thing fell apart by the end of the party. I hope this project will hold up a little better."

Doug laughed. "I still have the pictures from that day. Your face was speckled with the blue paint you put on the Styrofoam, and I was pulling splinters from the barnwood for a week. We made a great team."

The room stilled as the two looked at each other. Was this the reason I was supposed to come back to Twin Station, Jadey wondered? Was Doug meant to be the guy I end up with after all these years? Katie said Doug had never gotten over her, and Jadey had to admit that thought gave her heart the tiniest of wobbles.

But she couldn't rid her brain of the story Katie had told of their own whirlwind romance and marriage and the child he fathered with his cousin. The whole thing unnerved her, and she couldn't sort out her feelings.

But she also couldn't deny the attraction. She had had a crush on him for a couple of years before she got up the nerve to really talk to him in seventh grade. Once the ice was broken, they got along like old pals. They enjoyed the same hikes in the woods, fishing at the creek, hanging out at the mall, going to movies. They shared many of the same friends, laughed at the same jokes.

The moment of quiet between them was broken when Doug shoved his hands into his pockets and turned reluctantly to the door.

"I hate that I have to go to work. I'd rather hang around here and talk about your new kitchen. Seriously.

Let's get the group together again this weekend. Maybe see a movie?"

Jadey felt for a moment like she was still a teenager, hoping the cute boy would ask her out. How on earth does someone who works with words for a living feel at a loss for something to say? She finally stuttered something as he walked onto her front porch.

"Sure. That would be great. Have fun at work."

When the door closed behind Doug, Jadey slapped her forehead. Have fun at work? Oh my god how lame was that? Good lord, I'm fourteen again.

Her eyes once again focused on the stairs and her mind returned to the realization this town had a lot of secrets. More than she could have imagined.

Chapter 11

The noise level at the auto repair shop rose and fell in a constant crashing sound, followed by the kind of lull where you hold your breath, anticipating the next crash. Doug and Ray routinely shouted over the noise to communicate with each other, and sometimes continued to shout out of habit, even when the machines sat silent.

The younger of the two, Doug handled most of the body work, removing dented quarter panels, replacing head lamps and tires, and repairing scratched and rusted rocker panels. Ray was the engine guy, with a head for computers and a huge investment in an array of diagnostic equipment. He was able to reset or replace almost any of the dozens of systems controlled by twenty-first century technology.

Both brothers had quit their jobs to buy the garage at a bargain-basement price when their neighbor retired after forty-five years in the repair business. But they borrowed heavily to build up the inventory of parts and specialized equipment to repair cars, and they both worked long hours, looking toward the day when they could actually realize a profit. They had one full-time employee who handled bookkeeping, the phones, and scheduling.

Doug and Ray were lucky they loved what they did for a living because they did it an average of ten hours a day, six days a week. Sundays were the one day they gave themselves to recover and rest.

At 5:30, Ray was preparing to head home after his own nine-hour day. Since Doug's shift began at 4:00 p.m., the two brothers used their overlapping work time to complete projects requiring the two of them, and to talk about the business and strategize. Sitting at a cramped counter in the small office in the back, wolfing down sandwiches and looking over the ad they prepared to place in the local paper, Ray coughed in surprise when police chief Howard Dent stopped in.

Dent made up for his physical imperfections with a louder-than average voice, his former drill sergeant days coming in handy when he used his vocal cords to broadcast who was in charge. Ten months out of the year, he kept a handkerchief in one hand to wipe the ever-present sweat from his upper lip, and absent-mindedly kept his other hand resting on his holstered Glock.

"Ray. Doug. Your faces are usually buried in a car engine. Come up for air?"

"Just about to go home, myself." Ray responded. "Doug and I are biting the bullet and putting an ad in the Sunday edition."

"What's this I hear about you getting a little too chummy with the Evans girl?" Dent directed his question to Doug, who froze with a bite of sandwich in his mouth.

Ray looked from the chief to his brother, a question in his eyes.

"I'm not getting chummy. Jadey and I are old –" A sharp slap across the face cut his sentence short as Dent's steely hand knocked the food from Doug's mouth and sent scraps of lettuce and lunchmeat flying. Both Doug and Ray recoiled at the sudden violence, with Doug's hand automatically going to his stinging cheek.

"What the...? What'd I say?" Doug stammered while standing up and backing out of Dent's reach. "I knew her back in high school. What's the problem?"

"The problem," Dent dragged the words out slowly for clarity, "is that bitch is the granddaughter of Ellie Evans, and we have no idea why she's here or what she's after. She starts making new friends, or reacquaints with old friends, and she just might start hanging around for a while. And that would be a problem for us, wouldn't it?"

Dent's hard eyes flashed between both of the Baylor brothers, challenging them to defy him. Doug reluctantly nodded, still favoring his sore cheek and his wounded pride. Ray looked at his brother, and then back at the chief. He hesitated for a second and then spoke up.

"Maybe it's a good way to figure out exactly what her plans are to have Doug keep tight and close." Ray wanted to add more, but stopped to see what kind of reaction his words had on the chief. Dent looked directly at him, sending a chill through Ray. After a minute, Dent backed up a step, putting an extra foot of distance between himself and the brothers.

"You might have something there, Baylor. Keep your enemies close, right?"

He turned his face to Doug, who wouldn't make eye contact, keeping his head down, eyes studying the top of the desk.

"This is what's going to happen, Dougie. You're going to keep close tabs on your little friend, find out what she knows, and give me regular reports. But don't think for a minute the Evans girl is going to be some kind of soft place for you to land. There are no soft places, right? Mission first."

Dent stared at Doug's head until he got a quick nod from the younger Baylor brother.

Satisfied, Dent turned toward the door, but stopped short before opening it. Without turning back toward them, Dent issued an uncomplicated command. "Find out what she knows and give me a report. It shouldn't take more than a couple of days."

Neither Baylor watched Dent slam his way out of their office. After a minute Doug spoke quietly.

"I told you he was a psychopath."

Chapter 12

The options in Red's Hardware Store were limited, but Jadey was happy to see they had a floor buffer for rent. The owner of the store wasn't overly friendly, which seemed odd considering she was paying money to rent a machine that looked like it hadn't left the shop in a year, but she decided she didn't need friendly, she just needed the machine.

With some amount of trouble, the two of them loaded the buffer into the trunk of her car, tying the gaping trunk lid to the bottom with some twine so it wouldn't bounce up and down on the trip home.

Home. She found she had been subconsciously calling it home again. It certainly had been home for all of those years until she was fourteen, but so much had happened in the meantime, and so many hurtful words had been thrown around, she lost the habit of referring to her grandma's house as home. But here she was, driving a car with the trunk wedged open, preparing to buff the hardwood floors at *her* home.

Lost in her thoughts, she started when she realized a squad car with lights flashing had pulled up behind her. She looked down at the speedometer to see if she had been speeding, but on this residential side street, pushing the thirty-mile-per-hour limit would be a challenge at any time. If anything, her care with the gigantic machine in her trunk had her creeping along under the limit.

She pulled to the side of the road, crossing her fingers and hoping the patrol car would pass her and head on to another destination, but unfortunately it stopped at the curb behind her. She couldn't see in the rear-view mirror because of the open trunk, but her sideview mirror gave her a good look at the officer driving the car. She realized she was a little disappointed he wasn't Dillanian.

She hadn't yet met Howard Dent, but she had gotten a good look at him at the Bag O' Bones the other night. Plus, his car had a distinct "Chief of Police" decal on all four sides. She sighed as he let her sit there for a minute while he casually called in his traffic stop over the radio. Eventually, he pulled himself out of the car, using the door itself as a means to leverage his extra girth from the low-riding Crown Vic. He took his time walking to Jadey's car, where she already had her window open and her driver's license in her hand. She sat in silence, waiting for him to speak first.

"Have you been pulled over so many times you know the drill?" He pointed to the driver's license she was already handing him.

"No, but I watch some TV. You can learn a lot from old episodes of *Law and Order*."

Dent kept a fake smile pasted on his mouth, but a little twitch in his eyebrow gave away his irritation. He made a point of studying the license and looking back up at her face.

"Says here your hair is blonde."

Jadey sighed.

"Blonde is really just a state of mind, don't you think?"

Dent gave her a hard stare. No answer. Jadey stared back at him.

"Was I speeding?"

Dent didn't answer, but instead went to the back of her car and played with the give on the trunk lid.

"You should have used a stronger piece of rope for this," he called back at her. "The twine doesn't do shit for keeping the lid from bouncing up and down. It's dangerous to be driving without complete control of what's happening to all parts of your vehicle."

Jadey opened the car door and swung her legs out, standing up and looking back at him. When she met him at the back of the car, she gave some tugs on the twine and found it was still holding fast. The lid hadn't been bouncing in the few blocks she had driven from the hardware store.

"This twine is what the shopkeeper gave me to hold it. I only have a mile and a half to go, and I kept to the side roads."

"Well now, that's not the point, is it?" He pulled a ticket book from his back pocket and flipped to the next blank page. "We're big on safety here in Twin Station. Things that come flying out of trunks can cause great damage to vehicles and people who might be following behind."

She eyed the ticket book, watching to see if he also pulled out his pen.

"I understand. We tied it pretty tightly back at the shop, and I was driving very slowly. And until you came along there was never a car or bike rider behind me."

Dent's eyes turned icy. Jadey felt her heart pound as she realized her mistake.

"The improper securement of the things in your trunk was what caught my eye. Your attitude is what's going to get you a ticket." He started to copy information from her driver's license into the top lines of the blank ticket.

"If I'm already going to get a ticket for attitude, then I feel free to add that I think you're full of shit. There's nothing improper about the way this lid is tied down, and both the shopkeeper and I tested it before I took off. What's the real reason you pulled me over?"

Dent gave Jadey a slow look from head to toe. His face was becoming purple from his attempt to restrain his anger. Jadey knew she had stepped in it.

"How long do you plan to stay in town, Miss Evans?"

That question again. She understood a bit of curiosity, but now two police officers and one old friend had asked her if she was staying. The hairs on the back of her neck stood up, and she rubbed her arms to remove the chill.

"I'd say it's none of your business, Mr. Dent. I own the house and I'll stay as long as I please."

Dent gave her a patronizing smile. He finished writing her ticket and tore it from his book.

"That's CHIEF Dent. And everything in this town is my business."

Chapter 13

The Twin Station Police Department was part of a larger Civic Center building the town paid dearly to build ten years ago. Previously, all of the city offices filled the upper floor of a department store that had gone out of business during an earlier recession, and those upstairs offices, with slit-style windows and poorly working air conditioning, had been like Hell to work in, minus the trip in on the River Styx. The police station threatened to burst through the walls of the lower half of the same building, and their air conditioning didn't work any better. City employees, and the people they were related to or knew, made up a large portion of the town, so when the vote to finance a new building made it to a referendum ballot, they had no problem getting a large enough response. This in spite of a recession that had the people in town and surrounding area walking around in a persistent butt clench.

Digital clocks throughout the building were in in sync, and read 12:30 p.m. Half the detectives were at lunch, most of the uniformed were on patrol, and even the chief was out in his specially-marked squad car. Greg Dillanian sat at his desk, poring over a file he kept only on his personal laptop. No paper trail, and no way anyone could access it without the password he kept in his head.

Reading through his most recent notes, he whispered a quiet expletive. His thoughts turned to the newest town resident and the worry burned in his throat. She's going to fuck things up. We're this close and if she gets any hint of what's happening, she's going to ruin all of this planning.

Hell, I'm going to have to stop her myself.

A buzz from his cell phone interrupted his thoughts, and a number he knew well showed on the screen. He sighed, and then reluctantly picked it up and touched the phone icon.

"Dillanian."

The voice on the other end asked if he would accept a call from Kurt Dillanian and, although he hesitated for a brief moment, he answered, "Yes."

His brother's voice was loud, as he shouted over a mix of background noise.

"Greg. What's happening, Bro? How's the world of the free and the brave?"

"Hi, Kurt. Things are fine here. How are they treating you?"

The call began with a routine they both found comfortable. Kurt pretended things were just fine in prison, and Greg pretended he worried about him. They talked for five minutes about sports and fishing memories before Kurt got to the reason for his call.

"Hey, I'm hoping you can come up for a visit sometime soon. You know I'm in a program to transition when I'm released, and I've got some questions for you. I'm going to need a job and a place to live, and since Mom and Dad are gone, you're the only one I can ask for help." Kurt paused. "It's a pretty big deal that I'm asking for help, isn't it? It's one of the things they're trying to encourage us to do. You know, reach out to family."

Kurt's voice shook a little, the emotion revealing itself.

Greg was sympathetic, but cautious. He made himself sound upbeat.

"How about I come up in a couple of days? I'll make the arrangements with the prison for a visit and we'll talk. I've already had some thoughts about this, and I wanted to get your take anyway. Do you need anything?"

"Nah, not really. Can you bring another bag of Mounds bars like you did last time? I ate most of the last ones, but some of them bought me into a couple of poker games."

"Sure, I can do that. I'll see you soon. Hang in there."

"Always do, Bro. Always do."

Chapter 14

It was already dark outside, and Katie swore at the front door. Where was he? She stood in her prettiest nightgown and looked at the two glasses of wine she poured an hour ago. One was nearly empty. Was he having trouble sneaking out, or did someone see him coming to her house and made him change his mind? Another half hour passed before she finally heard his car in the driveway. The headlights dimmed, but she didn't hear the car door open.

Again, her thoughts turned to confusion. Normally he practically had his pants off by the time she let him in, he was so eager. What's the matter? She risked a look between the drapes and could see by the moonlight he was sitting in his car, thinking or listening. Was he on the phone? She couldn't tell.

Damn it, just get in here, she thought. I've been sitting here for over an hour now. Maybe we'll skip the wine and go right to bed. Or the shower. He loved what she did to him in the shower.

Another five minutes went by before she heard the car door open, and then close, and then heard his footsteps on the front door mat. She tried to look casual, wine glass in hand, when he entered the house and stared at her. She could tell that something was wrong by the look on his face.

"What is it sweetie? What's wrong?"

"I think you know what's wrong."

Her mind flashed with thoughts, confused. Did I forget something? I didn't give away our secret, did someone find out? What the hell?

"No. I don't know. Did something happen at work? Are you hurt?"

He strode over to her, his eyes dark and dangerous.

"You're hanging out with the wrong people, Katie. At the Bag 'O Bones, I saw who you were with."

Katie pictured the scene. She was at a table with her old friends. He acted like he had caught her with another man.

"You know I still see Doug, just as a friend, right? Right? And Chad and Jeanie, just old high school friends."

"It's the half-blood I'm talking about. How humiliating for you to show up in public with the likes of her. What were you thinking?"

Katie could tell her lover had come in angry and was getting angrier. She had to think of just the right words to bring him back down.

"Jadey is just an old friend too. From high school. We go all the way back to grade school. You knew about her. We were just ..."

She never got the rest of the words out because he leaned in and suddenly grabbed Katie by the shoulders, slamming her up against the wall. The back of her head hit with a resounding "crack" and she felt her eyes roll back. Struggling to still talk, to explain, she found herself mumbling, and then his big, sweaty hand covered up her mouth, making it hard to breathe.

"Just shut up and listen. This is how it's going to be. The only time you will see the Evans bitch is when I tell you to, and that will be when I want some information. You're not going to suddenly start baking cookies together, or go shopping. Do you understand?"

Katie nodded her head, desperate to get his hand off of her mouth.

"When you do as I tell you, you get rewards, right? You give me what I want and I give you something as a treat. You don't talk to the Evans girl unless I tell you to."

Katie nodded again, her eyes darting back and forth, looking for a way out.

Satisfied with her answers, he took his hand from her face and used it to unzip his pants.

"Now get down on your knees and give me what I came for."

She slid down along the wall to her knees and fumbled with helping him pull his pants down to his knees.

"Make it a good one, Katie. You don't want me mad at you."

Chapter 15

For the third time, Jadey stared into the safe room behind her grandmother's closet. The feel was otherworldly, as if she found herself on the set of a horror movie, where the innocent victim had to create a safe haven from some source of evil. But who was the evil in her grandma's life? What had her so frightened she went to such lengths to protect herself? There had to be something, somewhere else, some other information, about what was going on. She blinked back tears. *I need to know what was happening here!*

She straightened suddenly, thinking there was some kind of clue and she just hadn't stumbled on it yet. Grandma's journals. The missing ones. She had them in her mind as she picked through some of the things in the house, but so far the only things close were some notepads where Grandma Ellie had scratched gardening supply lists and reminders about important dates. Grandma would have turned to her journals for something this unusual. Absolutely. It didn't solve the problem of where they were, but Jadey felt more urgency to search.

She flew down the stairs to the main level and headed for the small living room. The space reflected her grandma's tidy-but-lived-in look. The shelves overflowed with her grandma's favorite books, and a basket in one corner held a knitting project; paused, waiting to be finished. A stack of magazines threatened to topple from the coffee table, but the rug was cared for, and the curtains looked like they were fresh from the cleaners. She took a moment to survey the room, picturing her grandma everywhere. She could see her fussing with the curtains as she pulled them back every morning. Picking up yesterday's newspaper from a pile next to her rocker. Wiping at the circle of coffee her mug left, before it could leave a permanent stain.

Thinking about the plots in her favorite thriller movies, Jadey headed to the bookcase.

If Grandma wanted to hide something, she thought, how about hollowing out the inside of a book? Maybe a key to a safe deposit box? The prominent spot, front and center on the bookcase, featured her own novel. Based on the obvious signs of handling, her grandmother clearly read it more than once. Jadey picked it up and flipped through it quickly, hoping her grandma had used her book as the safe hiding spot for whatever information she might have hoped to keep safe.

Nothing. No hole cut out of the body of the book. No slips of paper pressed between the pages. Too obvious, Jadey realized, and she felt silly for even thinking of it. There was no chance her grandma would have cut up her book for any purpose anyway. The last time the two had talked, Jadey had laughed, and cried "Stop. Stop!" with the grand praise her grandma had had for her. She was being overdramatic, Jadey decided. Her book would be the last one that Grandma would have cut up.

Her eyes scanned the books on all of the shelves, looking for some hint of one Grandma would choose for a special purpose. The light dust on the shelves didn't give a hint that any volume had been pulled out recently, and no title jumped out at her as any kind of clever hint. She sighed, looking at the job ahead of her, and then started with the books on the top shelf.

An hour and a half later, Jadey stretched out on the floor, her neck and back muscles aching. The stacks of books surrounded her, every one of the books getting the same flip-through treatment she gave her own novel. She again laughed to herself realizing she probably had too great of an imagination. She didn't even have any specific reason to believe her grandma had hidden anything, or that she would have used such a cliché method.

Except for the safe room. It existed.

Exhausted, she tried to rethink her strategy. Maybe the safe room was just some kind of hyperactive inventiveness on the older woman's part, or extra caution in preparation for some weather disaster. Maybe she just got bored and thought it would be fun to see if she could create a secret room. Her grandma definitely had been a woman with a quirky sense of humor and an affection for adventure.

Jadey looked around the room, now a major tripping hazard. She tried to brush off her worries, talk herself out of the fear that nipped at the base of her skull. But she couldn't seem to shake the feeling in her gut that all was not as it seemed. She had learned long ago to trust her instincts, and right now they were telling her to keep looking.

Chapter 16

Sergeant Greg Dillanian stood outside Chief Dent's office and caught his attention when he returned. The chief appeared angry and distracted. Sweat soaked the armpits of his uniform, and even the normally taut navy-blue tie hung at an angle.

"What do you want? I've got a meeting with the mayor in ten minutes."

"I think we need to talk about our newest citizen. The Evans girl."

Dent's head snapped up at the mention of Jadey Evans.

"What about her?"

Dillanian moved in closer, lowering his voice so it wouldn't carry into the room where officers were busy on their phones, or talking with civilians.

"I think she's kind of a troublemaker. Seems like the type to be asking a lot of questions."

Chief Dent reached into his mini-fridge for a bottle of cold water and plopped down in his special-order desk chair. It cost the taxpayers $2,000 but he hid the expense as tactical police equipment cost. He eyed Dillanian and paused before speaking.

"What do you know about her?"

"Not much. She doesn't have a police record anywhere in the country and, except for a couple of juvenile pranks, I don't see her being a problem for law enforcement. But I see her being a problem with everything else."

The unspoken suggestion hung in the air between the two men.

Dent looked out his window, thinking. Finally, "I agree. I've been thinking the same thing."

"I want to get a little closer," Dillanian suggested. "See if I can get a hold on what she knows, if she's got some kind of intention here. We have no idea what her grandmother told her."

"We didn't find anything when we searched her place when we … when she was found. But I just have this crazy gut feeling she was keeping notes. She was kind of a meticulous old bitch, and a little birdie told me she used to write shit down. Somewhere."

"I agree." Dillanian turned to leave the room.

Dent stopped him at the door. "When's your brother getting out?"

Dillanian knew the chief was keenly aware of the exact date his brother would be released from prison.

"Six months."

"I think we could find a way to use him. Have him get in touch with me."

Dillanian turned the subject back to Jadey.

"Permission to make contact? Try to establish some rapport to feel her out a bit?"

His boss curled up the corner of his mouth in a sweaty leer. "Maybe feeling her out would be a fun way to get some information. She IS a looker, that girl, even if half of her comes from putrid stock."

Without responding, Dillanian left the office, determination in his step.

Chapter 17

The only room Jadey hadn't entered yet was her mom's bedroom. She wasn't sure what kept her from opening that closed door at the end of the hallway, but she found herself always making excuses to check it later. Some other time. There's always tomorrow. Eventually. Her thoughts usually didn't progress any further. But now, her mind clicked off the possibilities: either the room was completely empty, knowing her grandma's animosity toward her mom, or it had been converted into a guest room, or was just used for storage. Her gut told her the sight of the room would be painful. Either way she managed to keep putting off going in. Until now.

Again, she admitted to herself she lived life with an overactive imagination, but her quest to find some secret notes or documents had put her in secret-agent mode. Jadey had gone so far as to fully scour the lower level. She removed pictures from walls, pulled out furniture to look behind it and under it, and even checked the bookcase for sliding compartments or hollowed shelves, before she replaced the books. So far, no sign of any clues to the story behind the safe room.

She stared at the closed door at the end of the hall. I'm going to have to see what's in there.

Her chest tightened a bit as she watched her own hand reach down. Chastising herself for the drama, she put her fingers on the knob and turned it.

Chapter 18

Nine miles out of Twin Station, a group of eight men stacked wooden boxes in the back of an old machine shed. They piled them five high, and each box carried a label with a giant stamp: **_Remington ACR_**. Through a very convoluted series of truck interceptions and extremely clever mockups of invoices, these army-owned selective-fire weapons found their way into the hands of a group of white nationalists known as The Clear Order. As disciples of Hitler, the shirts they wore and the scrawled "artwork" on the walls of the machine shed carried symbols of the Nazi regime. The boxes full of weapons gave testament to the fact The Clear Order members had access to many more lethal tools than any of Hitler's civilian fans when Nazis ran Germany.

Twenty feet behind these newly stacked piles, tarps covered another ten, hiding within them enough rifles to kill thousands of people. The all-but-certain stampede of terror would kill or injure more.

In another, smaller shed, ammunition stored in wooden bins, along with smoke bombs and hand grenades, completed their arsenal and evidence of deadly intent.

The sheds were what remained of an old tool-and-die making business, begun by Samuel Kingman in 1955. His son Will joined the family business in 1969 and the two enjoyed a busy, if not entirely lucrative, small enterprise. Quite adept in their trade, they enjoyed the respect and influence as members of the Twin Station community. Samuel and Will lost their lives in the now infamous flood of 1972 when unprecedented rainfall overwhelmed the town's sewer system and created rising waters filled with whatever could float. Teams of people waded and canoed through the residential parts of town, searching for stranded residents and helping them escape to higher ground. Samuel and Will went under together when a car, lifted from its parking space a block to the north, drifted in the waning hours of daylight and crushed the two against the home of an elderly woman who had hung a white towel out of her window, signaling for help.

Without her husband or son, and with her own home uninhabitable because of the flood, Samuel's wife, Catherine, abandoned her home and her husband's business, and moved to her brother's home in Michigan. Local firefighters, worried the structure had become unsafe, tore down the principal building of the tool and die shop decades ago, but the sheds hung on for dear life. The thirty-acre plot, surrounded by forest, had long been the property of an investment company which made money buying abandoned lots in rural areas, and then selling them at inflated prices to people or businesses that wanted to develop the space. They had many properties in their portfolio, which was good, because finding buyers often took a decade or more. This one stood abandoned for seventeen years.

The isolation made it an ideal location for a group of people who required subterfuge and secrecy to organize. Almost invisible from the highway, spreading trees and undergrowth had long ago crept over the dirt driveway that opened to the flat parcel. From the road, you had to know the driveway was there or you would miss it. Once through the thick foliage, people intent on creating chaos could go about their business, with people in passing cars completely unaware.

On the perimeter of the grassy property, ten vehicles of various makes and sizes sat idle. Jeeps, vans, sedans, and small trucks made up a ragtag fleet of nondescript vehicles that would never catch the attention of law enforcement. The trunks and back seats would be adequate to deliver rifles and ammunition to their intended destination, but for now, they sat empty. The inventory of arms and ammo in the sheds would be a signal of a flash-bang announcement to the world that The Clear Order had arrived.

Chapter 19

Jadey felt the knob turn easily in her hand and after a second's pause, she pushed the door open and stepped inside. She felt herself sway for a moment as the stunning sight made her blink and hold the door for support.

Grandma left her mom's room completely intact, her bed made up with the same comforter and pillows Jadey instantly remembered from her childhood. The dresser was in the same position between two windows along one wall, and a small table and chair remained where her mom sat to apply make-up and fix her hair. Familiar yellow-and-blue curtains hung from windows overlooking the back-yard.

But what really stunned her were the pictures. Where there had been no pictures of her mom in the other rooms of the house, this room was filled with them. Baby pictures. Elementary school class pictures. Photos of her mom clinging to a tire swing in the backyard. A separate display of her high school graduation picture stood alongside one of her in the princess court for homecoming.

Pictures in frames covered the walls and filled the top of the dresser. Around them, little things her mom had left behind when the two of them had fled. She recognized the costume jewelry and a vase filled with some cheap, plastic flowers her mom had gotten such a kick out of. The displays were like an homage. Grandma had created the room as a place to celebrate her only daughter.

Jadey felt tears running down her cheeks and she wiped them away with the palm of her hand. When she lowered herself to sit on the side of her mom's bed, her eye caught another picture on the nightstand. In it, her seventeen-year-old mom's face was lit up with a smile, and she was caught in the embrace of a young Black man, the love of her life. Here, finally, a picture of Joe. Jadey's father.

She fingered the picture for a moment, trying to memorize every feature of the young man her mother loved. "Grandma, you're still just full of surprises, aren't you?" she said to the room. "I'm more confused than ever. What happened between you and Mom?"

Jadey stretched out on her mom's old bed, snuggling on the worn, but cheery comforter, sniffing the pillow hoping for a hint of her mom's favorite perfume. She must have lain there, trance-like, for several minutes, when the ringing doorbell interrupted her thoughts.

Quickly jumping up from her place on the bed, she backed out of the room, closing the door firmly behind her. By the time she reached the bottom of the stairs, she wiped her face clean of the tears and raked her fingers through her hair, but her heart was still reeling from the discovery upstairs.

"Oh. Gosh. Hi."

She stumbled over what to say when she saw Greg Dillanian on her front step. Their last encounter had been weird, with him showing up in her backyard as she lugged chunks of drywall to the dumpster. She and Katie had talked about him, and in the past couple of days she found her thoughts occasionally drifting to him, embarrassed by how attracted she could be to someone who was little more than a complete stranger. Here he was. Looking back at her.

"Do you have time to talk?" he asked simply. No hello. No smile. Just the blunt request and, since his words came out with the voice and the badge of a police sergeant, the question felt almost like an order.

"Sure. I mean, time is kind of your friend when you work freelance."

"Sorry, did I interrupt your writing?"

"No, no, not at all." Shrug. "Even my demo work is freelance, I guess. I'm on a two-month self-imposed hiatus from writing. Recharging I guess."

She moved aside and let him in. His eyes took a big sweep of the living room, and then moved to the kitchen and dining room where the bare studs revealed her progress.

"You've been busy. Have you filled the dumpster yet?"

"Almost. I'm done taking down everything for this part, but I'm going to keep the dumpster for when I clear out the shed. It's so full you can't get another shovel in it."

"Both handy and creative. It makes you kind of interesting."

"I'll take 'kind of.' I can make coffee too. How do you like it?"

"Black is good." He stuttered for a moment. "I mean ..."

Jadey laughed. "Are you afraid you just stepped in something because I'm bi-racial? I get that all the time. It's okay to use the word black around me, you know."

Dillanian pulled at his collar. Didn't make eye contact.

"Sorry. No, I didn't mean anything. Yes, I'll have some black coffee."

She smiled as she turned to the makeshift table she created with a board resting on two sawhorses. Her coffeemaker and toaster shared the space with a loaf of bread and a canister of coffee grounds.

"What's up?"

He yanked his head in her direction.

"What do you mean?"

"You said you wanted to talk. What's up?"

Dillanian walked over to the window to stare at the side yard. "Nothing important. I just like to get to know everyone in town. I've been here almost a year and still there are people I've only passed on the street. It's just neighborly to know everyone. At least – people who might be planning to stay."

Jadey's skin prickled a little at the reference once again to whether or not she was permanent. She pretended to concentrate on measuring the coffee grounds so she didn't have to respond. Eventually, when she couldn't continue the pretense of a deep focus on the coffee machine any longer, she turned to face him.

"How long have you been a police officer? What's your story?"

"Not much to tell. After college I did two years in the Army and then joined a rookie class in the Columbia, Missouri Police Department. Put in eight years, and then last year I transferred here."

"What made you move from Missouri to Wisconsin? Do you have family nearby?"

"Just a change of scenery, I guess. I get stale if I stay in one place too long."

"You're kind of the cliché of a cop, you know. Short answers. Only the minimum amount of information shared. Face breaks if you smile."

He looked at her and couldn't help but chuckle.

"You probably nailed me. Old dog you know."

She filled two coffee cups and walked to where he stood by the window. She handed him his cup.

"If you react to sudden movements like the cops I see on TV, we may soon have coffee spilled all over us."

Focused on her target, Jadey leaned in, tilted her head a fraction, and put her lips against his. He didn't flinch. No coffee spilled. He kissed her back.

Chapter 20

When Jadey finally pulled back, Dillanian looked at her with a mixture of interest and yet distance. Jadey smiled, but looked down at her shoes.

"Sometimes I tend to do things a bit impulsively, without stopping to think it through first."

Dillanian tilted his head. "Does that ever get you into trouble?"

Jadey returned her gaze to look directly into his eyes. "I'd say pretty much all the time. But it also has its rewards once in a while."

A knock on the door interrupted the moment.

"Damn, what is it with people and their timing?"

She looked at Dillanian for a minute, chewing on her lower lip as she took in his face. Then she turned and walked to the front door.

She recognized the face of the older woman on the other side, and the moment felt like a déjà vu from when she had first opened her door to Doug Baylor. Memories of her childhood leapt into her mind. The face she knew, but she couldn't place the context.

"Jadey?" the woman asked. "My gosh, you've grown into a beautiful young woman."

The voice was familiar.

"Mrs. Sheridan! Oh my goodness how nice to see you."

"I've been meaning to come and say hi to you, but today when I saw the police car out front, I had to check. It scared me after what happened to your grandma."

Jadey invited Mrs. Sheridan into the house. The older woman stopped when she saw Dillanian standing at the kitchen window.

"Don't worry, Mrs. Sheridan. This is a friend of mine, Sergeant Dillanian. He just stopped by to talk." Jadey shot him a conspiratorial smile at the words.

"And I've got to get going. Hi, Mrs. Sheridan. I remember you from when I took a report on the day of Mrs. Evans' passing."

He strode to the front door and turned to Jadey before leaving. "Thanks for the coffee. And good luck with the kitchen remodel." Jadey stared for a moment at the door when he closed it behind him.

Once he left, Mrs. Sheridan took a moment to look around. "Oh my, you've been busy. I saw the day the dumpster arrived and wondered how you were going to fill it. A whole new kitchen coming. How exciting!"

"Thank you. I'm just hoping I'm not in over my head. It seemed like such a good idea when I started ripping things out. Grandma always hated the way the kitchen was oriented, so I think she'd approve."

"Back when our houses were built, they didn't think to open up a view from the kitchen to some comfortable seating where people could talk. And they sure never factored in dishwashers or wine refrigerators."

"I'm definitely going with the dishwasher. Not sure on the wine refrigerator. My idea of a glass of wine is a cheap white, mixed with Sprite and crushed ice. I definitely don't have a future as a wine reviewer."

Mrs. Sheridan smiled. "But you are a writer. Your grandma was so proud of you."

"Come on in and sit down. I may have destroyed the kitchen but I haven't broken up the furniture in the living room."

The two of them sat down, but Jadey jumped at her guest's whispered comment.

"I wonder if you've had the chance to look into whether Ellie was murdered."

Chapter 21

Work slowed where the men moved boxes of rifles and ammo. They pulled wooden crates and bins from the dark recess of the largest machine shed to a staging place in the front of the building. The work was hot, and the air was hard to breathe. The moving process stopped frequently with breaks to wipe sweat and take drinks of bottled water.

Among the men moving boxes were Doug and Ray Baylor, and Doug fought to hold back his anger.

"What the hell are we doing, Ray?" He kept his voice low, so the rest of the sweaty, gritty men wouldn't hear him.

"Shut up, Doug. You know exactly what we're doing."

"Well, maybe I'm done here. This isn't what I signed up for. No one told us we'd be storing up literally tons of guns and ammo. What the fuck is going on?"

Ray stood up and put his nose right up next to his brother's face. Doug didn't flinch, but his eyes gave away a note of fear.

"You've been seeing the same thing we've all been seeing. Our town, our state, our country, is being taken over by filthy vermin. We're being pushed out of our own country by people, by scum who don't belong here, who don't work for what they've got. They're takers, and they're trying to take what's rightfully ours. They will NOT replace us, but if we're gonna put things right again, it's gonna take firepower. We're done with letting 'em walk all over us."

Doug backed up an inch to put space between him and his brother. "There's gotta be another way. This is going to be nothing but a river of blood if we unleash all this stuff." He turned to look at the boxes all around them. "This is crazy shit, Ray."

Ray returned to grab another box and hoisted it on his shoulders.

"The real crazy shit is still ahead of us, brother. But when it's done, we're going to get back what's ours!"

Chapter 22

The security check at the entrance to the Minnesota Correctional Facility in Stillwater, Minnesota, was a familiar one to Greg Dillanian, but it never got any more pleasant. Stepping through those gates still felt like walking into a twilight zone of sorts. Knowing his own brother lived on the other side of the locks and heavy steel doors was a constant reminder of the path his brother chose in his younger life.

The exterior of the facility didn't suggest it housed a lock-up. The light brown brick and mini-blind windows facing the street looked much the same as many office buildings, or even housing complexes. The high security fence around the entire perimeter was a giveaway, but even that could have been mistaken for a secure manufacturing plant to anyone just driving through the area. A bank was open for business a block away, shady residential streets began just a couple of blocks further, and many other surrounding businesses all shared a view of the nearby St. Croix River.

The family visiting area was busy. People occupied most of the chairs, but Greg found a corner set of seats where they could talk to each other across a table, able to converse easily. The large bag of Mounds bars made it through security, and Kurt hugged it to his chest, the smile revealing his thanks.

The conversation began in the usual way with Greg asking if Kurt was okay, and Kurt shrugging it off as if he were living the dream.

"I'm really liking the woodworking shop, Greg. I think maybe I can make it as a carpenter. Really. They're good about the training, and I feel like maybe I was made for working with my hands, making things out of wood."

Greg leaned forward, always careful to keep the conversation just between the two brothers, but his sentiment was sincere.

"I've seen those pictures of the shelving units you guys made for an elementary school. Good stuff. I know they're pretty genuine here about helping guys transition with skills that will give them a real trade. Like I said on the phone, I've got a couple of contacts who might be able to help you out. You'd start doing grunt stuff of course, but once they see your woodworking skills, you'll move up fast."

Kurt nodded, but still unable to keep the sarcasm out of his voice.

"Course I'm never going to be a hot shot detective like my big brother. You know I still tell everyone here you're a baker. I wouldn't want to take a beating for having a cop for a brother."

"I wouldn't want you take a beating for any reason, Kurt. Just keep your own nose clean and I'll do the same. You get out in six months, so don't blow it."

Kurt turned away; his moods always subject to change at a moment's notice.

"I sure made Mom's life a mess, didn't I? She tried so hard to get me to be more like you, but no matter how hard I tried, I couldn't ... I could never fill your shoes, big bro."

Greg held his anger, having had this conversation many times over the years.

"Our mom told you a thousand times how much she loved you exactly for who you were, Kurt. No one is able to fill the shoes of an imaginary standard that existed only in their own head. I was never perfect; Mom and Dad weren't perfect. You spent your life thinking you had to reach some kind of ideal that no one ever set for you! Maybe when you get out of here, you can focus on just doing the best you can, staying clean, and enjoying the simple things, like heading to the lake on a weekend."

"That's the dream, I gotta tell you. You don't know how much you appreciate the little things until you've been locked up with a key that someone else is in charge of. Tell you the truth, the first thing I'm going to do is rent one of those bikes at Lake Harriet and just ride around and around for a couple of hours."

"I'll join you if you let me."

The two brothers shared a look across the counter. Greg finally broke the silence.

"I gotta get back to work. It's an hour drive and I still have a couple of reports to write up."

"Always on the job, man. You'll be working late tonight."

"Good to see you, Kurt. Focus on the prize. Six months."

Kurt smiled. "Six months. Sometimes I can almost taste it."

Chapter 23

"What do you mean, murdered? What are you talking about?"

Mrs. Sheridan leaned in toward Jadey, as if to be sure even the old house wouldn't hear her.

"There is no way your grandma fell down those stairs. She was as spry as a twenty-five-year-old, and you know that not a drop of liquor passed her lips. And it's not like she was carrying something big in her arms to cause her to fall. I saw her. I found her there. At the bottom of the stairs. There was nothing else there. Nothing she would have been carrying, or could have tripped on."

"But that's a long way from thinking it was murder! I mean, she could have turned to swipe at a cobweb or something, and just missed a step."

"It was no cobweb that killed my friend Ellie. She was getting too close to something, and they had to put an end to it."

Jadey looked at Mrs. Sheridan, confusion racing through her head. Perhaps the older woman had become a little bit addle-brained since she last saw her. Maybe this talk of murder was a sign of dementia. Yet those words grabbed Jadey's attention. *She was getting too close to something.*

Not wanting to raise alarm, she tried to steer Mrs. Sheridan to more rational thoughts.

"I'm sure there is an explanation, but with no one else here at the time, we'll never know for sure."

"But there was. There was someone else here. That's what I wanted to tell you, and why I was nervous when I saw the police car here today. The morning she died? There was a police car parked in the back of the house. I thought it was odd that it wasn't just in the driveway. I mean, I don't know why there would be police here at all, but why was the car pulled around the house to the back?"

Jadey grabbed the pillow on the couch and pulled it to her chest while Mrs. Sheridan talked.

"What are you saying? The police had something to do with her death? I don't understand."

"What I'm saying is Ellie was pushing the wrong buttons. She got too close to something and they had to shut her up. You think I've been watching too many weird shows on TV, don't you? Did your grandma tell you anything about her investigations?"

"No." Jadey sat stunned. "I don't even know what you're talking about." But maybe she did. The safe room.

Mrs. Sheridan stood up and walked over to the window. She was quiet for a moment, gathering her thoughts. Her voice trembled a little when she spoke.

"Have you noticed the town has an unnatural look about it? Like we don't exactly fit into the country overall? I'm talking about diversity." She paused. "I know you don't expect an old woman like me to be talking about things like diversity, but your grandma was a real woman of the world, even though she rarely left her home town."

Jadey nodded, understanding the reference. "I know what you mean. She rarely got more than two hundred miles from Twin Station. Barely more even when she took me on trips. But she was always an avid reader, of books, newspapers. She was more worldly thinking than most people I know."

"That's it. She was worldly thinking. She was always pointing me to articles in the *New York Times*, or even as far away as the *London Daily Telegraph*. She read everything she could get her hands on. So curious. And ultimately, so angry."

"What happened?"

"She started to notice a pattern, and I think it led to her death. Have you noticed yet how few people of color live in Twin Station?"

The question took Jadey by surprise. She looked at Mrs. Sheridan, confused.

"People of color? Like me?" She just shrugged, unsure where this conversation was going.

"That's right. Like you. Or like my dear friends Harold and Sonya. Theirs is the story we've come to recognize here. They moved here about eight years ago. Retired from teaching jobs. Both of them. I loved Sonya. She felt like a soulmate to me and it never mattered to either of us that our skin color didn't exactly match up."

Mrs. Sheridan stopped for a moment, collecting herself as her voice broke.

"Three years ago, Harold just suddenly disappeared. Just up and left, without a trace. It was so unlike him, and

Sonya was frantic by the time he'd been gone for about four hours. Fifty-two years of marriage and they barely spent a day apart, and here he'd left for a quick trip to the grocery store and never came back."

"Did she call the police?"

"Oh yes. She did. They took the report and made sounds about how they can't treat an adult as a missing person until he'd been gone twenty-four hours. You know the drill."

Mrs. Sheridan paused in her story. The room was quiet.

"By day three, Sonya was about to lose her mind. By then, the police had searchers out for a couple of days, and had contacted other police departments with his picture. But there was nothing. Never a single sign. Not a single clue. The police tried to tell Sonya he must have just decided to move on. Start a new life or some other hogwash. It was ridiculous. Anyone who knew those two knew there was a better chance he had hitched a ride on a rocket to the moon. Harold would never have left her. Voluntarily."

"What happened?"

"Nothing, sadly. The police wrapped up their fake investigation in two weeks and closed the books. They told Sonya there was nothing else they could do. She would have to accept he was gone." She finally moved last year, back to Milwaukee, where they lived before."

"What do you mean by 'fake' investigation? Was there reason to believe they didn't really look for him?"

"Hell yes! Excuse the French."

Mrs. Sheridan came back to sit by Jadey.

"That's what I've been trying to tell you. It's what Ellie was looking into. This didn't just happen to Sonya. Black men have been disappearing for years, now and again. Or if they didn't disappear, Black or Asian families who had been settling in here just up and moved away, without a word to anyone. Something really strange, and so awful, is happening in Twin Station, and your grandma made it her purpose to find out what it is."

"And you think she was killed for that?"

"I know it. With every fiber of my being, I know it. Ellie was killed, because she got too close to the truth. What they don't know is Ellie wrote it all down."

Chapter 24

"She wrote it down." Not a question. It confirmed what Jadey knew in her gut. Something happened here and her grandma kept notes, and then hid them. As soon as she discovered the safe room, she knew something frightening happened in this house, and her instincts told her Ellie Evans would have recorded it.

"Do you know where she kept her journals? I was actually looking for them because ..." Jadey couldn't finish the statement. Her throat caught with fear.

"You haven't found any?" Mrs. Sheridan was surprised. "I know she wouldn't have left them just sitting out, but have you looked in her dresser? Closets?"

"I just found some old ones, but nothing recent. The first place I looked was in this room. In these bookshelves. I thought if she was going to hide them, she might have tucked them behind some books or something, but I took everything down and didn't find them."

"So, you've felt it too. That something was really wrong here."

"I guess I did. Some things just didn't feel right." Jadey wasn't ready to talk about the safe room. "I figured she would have written about it. So I started looking for her journals, here, in her bedroom, even in my old room and my mom's. I know they weren't in the kitchen because I tore everything in there down to small pieces. I haven't looked much in the cellar, but just a quick glance looked like she just stored some old broken chairs and some tools down there."

Mrs. Sheridan stood up to leave. "Keep looking. She wouldn't have trusted them with anyone other than me, and since I don't have them, I'll bet they're still here. Just be careful. The police sergeant who was here when I came looked nice enough, but Ellie's instincts pointed in the direction of our police department. And I can't get the picture of that police car out of my head on the day she died. It was here in the morning, but then Ellie was left for me to find."

Mrs. Sheridan wiped a tear that found its way onto her cheek.

"I don't want anything to happen to anyone else in this town."

Chapter 25

Ten minutes after Mrs. Sheridan left, Jadey grabbed an overnight bag, filled it with the things she needed for one night and headed out to her car. As she opened her car door, she noticed a patrol car turning the corner a block away, heading in the other direction. A chill went up her back. Were they watching her? Did they think she knew whatever dark secret her grandma had kept?

She pulled the car door shut and put her key in the ignition. What was the real reason Dillanian came by to see her today? Is he watching her too? If the police played any part in harming her grandma, who was in on it?

A little faster than she intended, she backed her car out of the driveway and headed toward the highway. Her eyes drifted to the fuel gauge and she saw she still had nearly a full tank of gas, but the thought brought her up short again. What was Dillanian writing in his logbook when she drove away? Dammit – she kissed him. He was interesting, damn good-looking, maybe dangerous. Was he the one who pushed her grandma down the steps?

"Okay, settle down Jadey," she spoke aloud to herself in the car. "You don't even know she was murdered. It could all be Mrs. Sheridan's imagination. And the police? Killing a citizen? Over what? What could have been so horrible that she was a threat to them?"

She willed herself to be calm. Focus on the driving. Think things through before jumping to crazy conclusions.

The drive to her mom's place in the Twin Cities took a little over an hour, and she looked at her watch when she pulled in front. If her mom didn't run any errands after work, she would probably be getting home soon. Jadey sat in the car in front of the cute little mid-century bungalow home in Richfield, a suburb of Minneapolis, and found her mind drifting back to her teen years. She was so young when she and her mom fled Twin Station. Starting over in a new town, a new school, and a disjointed home life rattled Jadey. She already had a shield up when it came to dealing with her own mom, and the new city filled with strangers added to her feelings of isolation and anger.

She didn't want to dwell on it now. They worked most of it out over the years, and she found new friends at the high school, but she never got over the feeling of being a bit of a refugee from a volatile past.

Lost in thought, she barely noticed when her mom's Toyota turned the corner and pulled into the driveway. She could see the surprised expression on her mom's face at seeing her daughter at the curb. Jadey opened her car door and the two women met in the driveway.

"Hi, Mom. Sorry I didn't call. I just drove up on a kind of spur of the moment."

"That's okay. It's a nice surprise." She glanced down at Jadey's overnight bag. "Come on in. I put a small roast in the crock pot this morning, so I actually have something to offer you to eat."

Once inside, Jadey settled on a stool at the island the two of them added when they did a kitchen remodel about ten years before. Those were some of the few really happy memories, Jadey thought, as she remembered the fun she had demolishing the 1950's kitchen down to the studs. Nothing works better for a mopey eighteen-year-old than swinging a sledge hammer.

The destruction of the kitchen had not only turned out to be a giant catharsis for her, but it gave her the experience that made her current demo job almost seem routine. Her mom found a local electrician to do the wiring, and a plumber to take care of the new pipes for the sink, but Jadey took on most of the grunt work, from hanging cabinets, to tiling the backsplash. The fresh, new kitchen became their favorite room in the house from that point on.

Trish opened the refrigerator and placed a wine glass under the spigot of a box of white wine on the top shelf.

"One of these days I'm going to introduce you to wine in bottles, Mom. With corks."

"Nonsense," her mom grinned. "You're not turning me into a wine snob! And you drink white wine with Sprite in it – so no lectures!"

Jadey laughed at the true characterization.

"I should have stopped for a six-pack on the way in, but today, I'll drink almost anything. Pass me one of those wine glasses."

"It's good to slum it sometimes," Trish said, without any sarcasm in her voice. "What brings you back?"

Jadey couldn't bring herself to mention her fears quite yet. She chose a different subject.

"Remember I told you I've gotten together with my old friend Katie Holman? We had dinner with a couple of other old high school friends."

"She's got a hair salon now," Trish said, remembering Jadey's call. "It sounds like you had a good visit."

"She took one look at my ratty fingernails and offered to put me through the mysterious process of getting lovely, long, bright red nails. I told her if the day ever comes that I can't paint my own nails, she could just shoot me. It made her snort beer through her nose, but I'm pretty sure she was drinking a Diet Coke."

They both laughed, and then sipped their wine. Trish sat on the stool next to Jadey.

"Now tell me what's on your mind. It isn't like you to just jump in the car and drive for an hour on a spur of the moment. And you brought an overnight bag. How are things back in Twin Station?"

"I've got so much to tell you, Mom, but even more to ask. I think after another two or three glasses of wine I'm going to press you to finally answer some of my questions, but first I have to tell you about your old room. You are not going to believe it."

"Let me guess. It's been reduced to charcoal. She burned everything and then threw a dead rat on the floor just for good measure."

"Mom. It's a shrine. I'm not kidding. Your mom, my grandma, made a shrine to you."

Trish's mouth gaped open.

"She has pictures of you everywhere. All of your school pictures. That picture I always loved of you on a pony where you're hanging on for dear life, halfway out of the saddle. The clipping from the Twin Station paper when you won a fresh turkey at the Turkey Days Raffle, and the one from the Minneapolis *Star Tribune* when you got that seat on the Park Board."

"She had that article? I didn't even tell her about the Park Board." Trish shook her head and then stared into space.

"It's because you almost never talked to her. The two of you were always like two junkyard dogs, circling each other and watching for one to make a move so you could bite the other's ear off."

"Oh please. Not even close. More like grizzly bears."

"True. More like bears who had deep, deep grudges against each other, and neither one of you willing to give an inch and talk it out. And, by the way, neither of you ever talked to ME about it either, so I spent my entire childhood wondering what was wrong with my family. Half the time I was sure it was my fault. The other half I hated both of you for how idiotic you acted. Mom, I'm twenty-eight years old. It's time for me to know the family secret."

Trish blinked several times, fighting against tears. She took a long sip of wine.

"I'll tell you something else," Jadey continued. "Your whole room was dust free, Mom. She'd been taking care of it all these years. You know what was front and center among the pictures? You and Joe, sitting on some kind of park bench. Looking like two young people completely in love."

Her mother's face was ashen. Trish carefully set down her wine glass, her hand shaking just a little bit despite her attempts to steady herself. For a couple of minutes, she couldn't make eye contact with her daughter, but eventually she cautiously looked up.

"You're right. It's time. Let's get it all out and finally put it all behind us. We're both going to need another glass of wine. Maybe something stronger."

Chapter 26

"Is he in?" Officer Connors rushed past the sergeant manning the front desk at the Twin Station Police Department, not waiting for an answer before heading to Chief Dent's office.

He slowed as he approached the partially opened door, seeing Dent bent over some paperwork and not looking particularly happy about it.

"I think she headed out of town for the night."

Dent slowly lifted his head to stare at the officer for a moment.

"I assume you're talking about the Evans girl?"

"Yep. I was patrolling the area like you told me. I got there right when Dillanian was leaving and she had a visit from that neighbor, Mrs. Sherwin."

"You mean Mrs. Sheridan. How long did Mrs. Sheridan stay?"

"Maybe twenty minutes, or a half hour. When she left, she looked kinda upset, and walked pretty fast back up to her place. I didn't know she could move so fast, as old as she is. About twenty minutes later, Ms. Evans came out of the house with what looked like an overnight suitcase. One of them pink things with a bunch of zippers you can put just enough in for a one-night stay?"

"So, it looked like she was headed out of town?"

"What it looked like to me, unless she always brings an overnight bag when she leaves the house."

"How long ago?"

"'Bout an hour. I would have come in right away to tell you, but I got called to that vandalism at the bowling alley. We caught the two punks sneaking down the side road. Still had the spray cans in their hands. Idiots."

Dent tilted his head toward the door.

"Thanks for the report. You can leave."

Connors gave a kind of half salute, but Dent's head was already back in his paperwork.

After a minute, Chief Dent stood and stretched, pulling his belt up over his rounded gut, and headed into the hallway. Dillanian's door was closed, but the light was on. After a quick, single knock with his knuckle, Dent opened the door and eyed Dillanian at his desk. The sergeant set down a report he just printed and looked up at his visitor, who barked out a question.

"Any luck getting any closer to that Evans woman?"

"A bit. Not much. I stopped by today, giving the story about trying to get to know all of the residents, since I'm still relatively new here. We had some coffee, she asked where I was from, I tried to find out if she is planning on staying, but right then the neighbor knocked on the door. It was obvious she came to visit, so I took off."

"Nothing else then? No clue about what her angle is?"

"My impression so far is she doesn't have an angle. I think the story checks out. She's just here because her grandma left the house to her, and she wants to fix it up and then decide if she'll stay or sell. She seems pretty genuine."

"What about the neighbor? Was it the one who found her?"

"Mrs. Sheridan. Yes. She seemed excited to see Ms. Evans. Sounded like she hadn't seen her since she moved away as a girl. It looked like a reunion starting up, so I made an excuse and left."

Dent stared through the blinds of Dillanian's window, although the dark night made it impossible to see anything except the streetlight on the corner. After a minute of silence, he made up his mind about something and headed for the door.

"Good job. Give me a report when you learn anything new."

Dent didn't wait for a response. He pounded down the hall, reaching out to grab his hat from the hook on his door on the way out.

Chapter 27

Trish paced in the kitchen. She picked up her wine glass, and then set it down without taking a drink.

"I'm not sure I know where to start. I've pushed the memories back so far in my mind I almost can't remember exactly when it started. You may be surprised to hear this, but for a long time, when I was little, my mom and I were best friends. We baked cookies together, she read to me all the time, from books, and newspapers. Everything. She was always sharing things she heard in the news even though I probably had no idea what she was talking about. We used to do things like cut random pictures out of the newspaper and then take turns making up stories about the people in the pictures."

"That sounds like Grandma. Those are some of the same things she used to do with me."

Trish nodded. "Actually, in a way, you got the best of her. Remember, she was sixteen when she had me. The classic story of her parents forcing her to marry the boy who got her pregnant because they didn't want a scandal. But as I got older, I began to suspect something really awful, and it clouded everything. I think my mom and dad hadn't exactly been lovers when they were teenagers. I think my dad raped her."

Jadey looked up, startled.

"They were never in love. I could sense that even when I was little. And my dad was horribly abusive to Mom," Trish said. "Yelling, throwing things ... and when he got drunk, which was often, he'd hit her."

"I had no idea." Jadey crossed her arms in front of her, wishing what she was hearing couldn't be true.

"I put together enough pieces of the puzzle over the years to understand I was conceived from my dad raping my mom under the visitor stands at the high school football stadium. She never told anyone at the time. No one ever told anyone in those days. When she turned up pregnant, her own parents forced her to tell who the father was, but I'm sure she never revealed how it happened."

Trish looked out the window, remembering.

"Her parents forced them to get married, so they did. Just like that. She dropped out of school to take care of me, and he got a job at the shoe factory in Oakdale. They resented each other and, for obvious reasons, I was the living symbol of why their lives had been destroyed."

Trish paused, started to refill her glass but changed her mind. Jadey quietly waited until she was ready to continue.

"Obviously, at sixteen, my mom wasn't at all ready to parent a baby, who later became a toddler, who then became a stubborn child. She tried. I know she tried. But she didn't have the tools. Like I said, she read to me and things like that, because books and reading was what was already natural to her. But she was probably completely overwhelmed by what it took to raise a child. And all the while fending off cuts and bruises brought on by her own husband.”

“I’m sorry. I had no idea. It would seem natural, I guess, resenting such a tough childhood. Is that what tore you two apart?”

“No. What tore us apart is that she didn’t save me from my father.”

●●●●●

A dark car, with its headlights blacked out, slowly crept to a spot on the curb half-a-block from Jadey’s house. Inside, Dent, having changed into dark street clothes, sat watching. The house was dark. Jadey’s car was gone. He watched for any sign of her in the area. A few minutes later, another darked-out car pulled up behind him and Officer Connors, also dressed in black, pulled himself from his car. He had a shoebox tucked under his arm. Dent joined him on the grass and the two stood quietly, an unspoken plan to listen and wait. The nocturnal sounds of hunting owls and crickets broke the silence. The two quietly headed toward the back yard and stood next to the shed, their backs to each other to keep watch on all the territory around them. Two sets of eyes checked out every direction to see if anyone had noticed their presence.

●●●●●

“What do you mean, save you from ...?” Jadey suddenly grasped her mom’s meaning.

“He started visiting me in my room on my twelfth birthday. Before, he used to make lewd remarks about my body, my obvious signs of puberty, laughing when I was embarrassed about getting my period. It all made me feel so ashamed, and just so disgusted. I already hated him because of the way he treated my mother, but as a kid I didn't know what to do about it. I didn't know if all families were like that because I learned early on people acted differently in public than they do behind closed doors."

Trish finally sat down. Resigned to finishing the story.

"You have to understand, my father was barely more than a carbon-based lifeform who only came out of a drunken stupor long enough to hit my mother, or turn to me. At first, he just touched me in ways that made me feel really queasy. He gradually started having me touch him, and the episodes got longer and more involved. I wondered if mom knew what he was doing. Didn't she notice he would sneak out of their bed in the middle of the night and come to mine? I didn't dare say anything. You never knew what would set him off, he was so violent, and Mom took most of the punches. But finally, when he really hurt me and I couldn't stand it anymore, I told Mom.

I waited until the two of us were home alone. Dad had just left for work and he wouldn't be home for hours. I thought maybe Mom would listen to me and we'd pack up our things and leave before he could come home. I had some kind of fantasy of the two of us escaping and starting some happy new life. But that didn't happen. She didn't believe me. She said I must have dreamed it, or something. I think I went into a kind of standing-up coma or something—I just stood there and heard her deny everything I said, but her words were all mixed-up sounding in my head. It was like I was under water and her voice was all gurgly. I couldn't believe it."

"Oh, Mom, I'm SO sorry."

Trish looked at Jadey, a sad smile on her face.

"I grew up pretty fast at the age of twelve. I learned I had to fear my dad and I couldn't go to my mom for help. I pretty much just shut down everything for a while. I didn't hang out with my friends. I didn't enjoy any of the things I used to enjoy – my TV shows, my books. I just lived with this bottomless pit of despair.

But, all of a sudden, things changed when Dad took off. About a month after I told Mom, he just suddenly left. He didn't take much of anything but his wallet. He didn't even call in to work to let them know he wasn't coming. Mom told me he told her he had had it, was ditching us and the town and everyone he knew and just leaving to start over somewhere else."

Jadey's mouth hung open. "So, just like that he was gone? Out of your lives forever? I had heard the story about him walking away at some point, but I never heard anything about where he went."

"We never heard either. Mom just said she didn't care where he went. She was always healing from one bruise or split lip or something else, and I imagine she was just relieved he was gone. But our relationship never got much better. We never talked about him and or about what he did. We pretended to just move on as if everything was totally normal, but of course, nothing was normal. And I resented her so much for not protecting me. For not believing me. I truly thought she didn't love me, or she would have put me first."

"I can't imagine what you went through, Mom. And I'm sorry now that I was so angry at you for your relationship with my grandma. All I ever wanted was for everyone to get along."

Trish managed a painful smile.

"I know, and you deserved a calmer household. I really wanted to forgive my mom, but I just couldn't seem to do it. Still, I wanted you to have a relationship with her. By the time you came along, she was so ready to actually be a mom. She was no longer a teenage girl with a baby and an abusive husband. She had time, and she had so much to give. So, I welcomed the time you spent with her and I'm glad you had a good relationship with her. But I just couldn't knock down the wall I had built up over all those years."

Jadey shook her head. Both brushed away tears, and then Jadey stood up, walked over to her mom, who stood and faced her. Jadey wrapped her arms around her, grabbing on tight to the woman who had endured so much, and whispered in her ear, "I love you so much Mom. You are my hero."

●●●●●

Dent knew which doors didn't latch very well because he had been in this house before. He quietly crept through the kitchen door with Connors behind him, and they stood still again. Satisfied they had the house to themselves, they carried the box into the other rooms, intent on their objective.

Chapter 28

Exhausted and spent, Jadey lay in her old bed in her mother's house, thinking about the two different bedrooms that had been such important parts of her childhood. Her experience was in stark contrast with her mother's experience, and she thought about the way a bedroom must have been a place of horror when her mom was just a young girl. Now Jadey understood. She and her mom cried together that night, and it was somehow both the ultimate sadness, but also a moment of great clarity. She now knew her mom so much better. Growing up, she saw her mom angry and spiteful and stubborn, but she never saw her vulnerable. Jadey felt she couldn't possibly love her any more than she did right then.

But now, her thoughts switched to her beloved Grandma Ellie. How could someone ignore the cries of her child? She didn't believe her own daughter! She didn't get rid of the man who preyed on her daughter. She allowed him to leave on his own terms. Maybe her grandma wasn't the doting, loving caregiver she had believed her to be. Once again, Jadey found herself questioning her judgment of people.

Greg Dillanian. Why did he keep invading her thoughts at such odd times? Was she so wrong about him too? Maybe she was allowing her attraction to him to hide the possible truth. Maybe he and the rest of the police department had something to do with her grandma's death. When he returned her kiss, did he feel something too, or was everything she thought she saw and felt just fake? The instant pain inside reached down to her toes. How could she ever trust again?

She slept restlessly and arose before her mom came downstairs. Jadey poured her mom a cup of coffee and the two sat at the same table where family secrets exploded open the night before.

"Such a pretty morning makes it feel like last night's discussion never happened," Trish tilted her head toward her daughter.

"As sad and as frightening as it was for you to tell me, I'm so grateful you did. I feel like this giant black shroud that followed me around for years has, I don't know, not exactly disappeared, but now there are big openings in it. It's not so dark. I feel like I have control over it, rather than the other way around."

"I promise I thought I was doing what was best for you, by not telling you. I thought about it at different times over the years, but at first you were too young. Then I wasn't ready. Then I felt like the time had passed and it was better left unsaid. You've always known your mom wasn't perfect. Not knowing how to handle this with you was the prime example of how imperfect I am."

"If perfection was a criteria for being a parent, our species would have died out a long time ago."

Trish laughed. She cupped her hands around the hot coffee mug to soak in its warmth.

"Can I ask about Joe, Mom? It's another topic that has never been explained to me. It's always been obvious he was my biological dad, but I never knew him, and no one really talks about him. When I was younger, you used to mention him sometimes. You told me he was the love of your life, but then why isn't he in our lives? Why isn't he in mine?"

"We're going to really clear everything out, aren't we?" Trish asked. She looked at the wall, as if for help with the words. Her response was in little more than a whisper.

"The truth is, I'm not sure, and that hurts. It's another pain I have never completely gotten over. You'll notice I haven't exactly pursued any other relationships with men."

"I know. I always wondered why you didn't date. You're so beautiful – and talented. Were you ... did you worry about bringing men to the house when you had a young daughter because of what happened to you?"

"No, no, that wasn't it. If there had ever been a sign of anything remotely creepy about a guy, looking at you, or anything ..." She couldn't bring herself to finish the sentence. She shrugged.

"It's hard to explain. For the first few years I just kept waiting for Joe to walk through the door. I was sure he'd come back. He'd have to. He had a daughter to meet, and I was waiting for him. It's one of the reasons it took me so long to move us out of your Grandma Ellie's house, because I wanted Joe to know where to find us."

Jadey listened, not interrupting.

"I know it sounds like I was imagining some kind of storybook fantasy, but it was just something so perfect, so timeless with Joe. We shared the same dreams of life; we truly loved each other's company. We weren't like typical seventeen-year-olds at all. It all felt ageless. We felt ageless. And I thought we had all of the time in the world together.

"We both knew when I became pregnant, we'd accidentally set something in motion that was going to be really difficult. I was repeating the mistake of my own mom, but it was more than that. The town and the whole world were really different than the way it is now. People at that time would say things like interracial marriages were the devil's work, or just some kind of earthly abomination. We knew we were going to face some problems. Big problems. But we also knew with all of our hearts we could make it."

"Then why did he leave? What did he say?"

"That's the problem. He didn't say anything. One day, he just left for his summer job at the General Store, and apparently just kept going. He was on his bike, and for some reason he just kept riding. His parents were distraught too. They guessed that maybe after thinking about it, he wasn't ready to face the kind of backlash we were going to get from our neighbors, but we all thought he'd just spend the night somewhere and then come back."

"But he didn't?"

"No. And one day led to another. Every day I woke up thinking he'd be at my door again. My mom actually liked him. She was wonderful that way. She liked the way he treated me. Oh, he was such a gentleman, and so, so kind. After a few days, I felt sure something must have happened to him. I couldn't believe what his parents were saying – that he just couldn't face the things the people in town would say. We were in love. We had made plans for the future. He never would have just left without saying goodbye, and I can't believe he wouldn't have stayed to meet you."

"Did you check hospitals in the area? Ask the police?"

"His parents were hesitant to ask the police. People like them, at that time, didn't feel like they could turn to the police for help, you know? They reached out to family and friends in other towns, looked for any sign of contact with someone he knew. And yes, they checked with hospitals for miles around. After about a month, I think they stopped looking. Stopped waiting. But I never did.

His parents eventually moved back to a town in Illinois where they had family, and when you turned fourteen, you and I moved here. Even after we moved to the Twin Cities, I still found myself looking for his face. I thought maybe he'd moved to a big city where he could get lost in the crowds."

"So, let me get this straight." Jadey sighed. "By the time you were seventeen years old, you'd been molested by your father, estranged from your mother, abandoned by the love of your life, and left to be a single mother of a bratty daughter. Does that cover it?"

Trish laughed. "I never called you bratty. You were ... willful. And look at what an amazing woman you turned out to be."

Chapter 29

The sun was directly above her when Jadey drove back into the driveway at her grandma's house. Her house. Keep saying it. Her house. She still wasn't used to ownership, to having a house just for her. She grabbed the bag of takeout burger and fries, along with her purse and a large Diet Coke. She could get her overnight bag out of her trunk later.

She had already, in this short time, gotten into the habit of pulling as far up into the driveway as possible to have a direct beeline to the back door that led into the ripped-up kitchen. Juggling her purse, the bag of food and the giant container of soda, she slid her key into the lock and entered the kitchen.

As soon as she stepped into the room the hairs on the back of her neck came to attention. She paused, not making a sound. Was someone in the house?

Jadey very quietly set her things on the makeshift counter where the toaster and coffeemaker had been push-ed together to make room for a hammer, a cordless drill, and a bag of Fritos. She listened again in silence. After a minute, she shook it off, wondering if she were becoming overly paranoid. Mrs. Sheridan's theory that, not only was her grandma murdered, but the evidence pointed directly to the police, still shocked her, but there were so many things that made her brain hurt. Multiple people asking if she was staying gave license to her creative, fiction-writing brain to fabricate some crazy conspiracy theory. And now, here she was, imagining people lurking in her house. Worse yet, she had begun to suspect Dillanian as part of this vast, murderous plot.

She shook her head, but then remembered the journals, which were still missing. The coincidence was too weird. Why would the journals be missing, or hidden, if the story was nonsense? Mrs. Sheridan's version of events might have a grain of truth to it.

She felt a renewed desperation to do some more hunting. Where would her grandma have put the books full of secrets? Was this what she was going to call them now? She already demolished the kitchen, painstakingly took every book off the shelf in the living room and, when she found nothing there, lifted every cushion, looked under and behind everything, even taken pictures off the wall, thinking maybe her grandma had a wall safe. And then she did the same things in all three bedrooms upstairs.

While she was going through all of this in her mind, she downed the burger and soda. I've got to start thinking more like Grandma Ellie, Jadey realized. Grandma went to all the trouble to wall off part of her closet to build a safe room, so if she really wanted to hide her journals, she probably thought of something equally clever.

If she were going to be paranoid anyway, she might as well be smart-paranoid. This would be the start of a new

search, with an eye on places where Ellie could have created a hidden opening in a wall or floor.

But as her eyes darted around the demoed kitchen, she shuddered. Jadey still had a frightening sense someone had been in her house. Who else was looking for those journals? Oh god, she hoped they didn't find them first.

Chapter 30

Jadey sat across the table from Katie at Pete's Pub, a homey saloon that had been a part of Twin Station since before Twin Station incorporated as a town. Unnerved by the feeling someone had been in her house, she had called Katie to see if her friend would be available for a beer later in the day. Katie was noncommittal at first, but called Jadey back later to say she could join her.

The sound of white cue balls hitting solids and stripes created a constant backdrop for the chatter at the pub. There hadn't been a "Pete" for at least seventy years, but the place still looked and smelled like the small-town corner-bar the original Pete Swanson built. Booths covered in Naugahyde upholstery and Formica tabletops still lined the walls, and barstools flattened by decades of butts six nights out of seven were proof of a place popular by locals. The bathrooms hadn't been updated for thirty years, but the toilets still flushed, the sink still ran icy cold water, and the urinals still drained beer that had been passed through bladders. The clientele was content.

Fun-loving Katie seemed different when they met. At the Bag O' Bones, she had been silly, and cheerful. Tonight, she was quieter, antsy. She kept looking away from Jadey, as if afraid to make eye contact.

"What's wrong, Katie? Are you feeling all right?"

"Sure, I'm fine. Just, I don't know, distracted I guess." She shrugged her shoulders. "Tough day at work."

"Then you're at the right place. Because there's beer." Jadey lifted her mug and drank.

Jadey hadn't decided whether to tell Katie about her suspicions and fears, but the conversation took its own turn when Katie ordered a second round before they fully drained the first, and asked Jadey about her mom.

"She's doing pretty well. I just went home to see her and we had a good talk. I feel like I'm on a much better path. Maybe 'stronger footing' is the way I would describe it because we cleared up some things."

"I think when we're kids, we don't always understand the big picture," Katie replied. "I remember when you were out of the house, at school, or just hanging out, you were a lot of fun to be with. But when you were with your mom and grandma, you always seemed coiled for a fight."

Jadey rubbed the condensation from her beer mug. "That's probably a pretty accurate description. The air was always heavier at home than when I was out with friends, or at school. And it didn't really get a lot better when Mom and I moved to the Cities and had our own place. I was such an angry kid inside. It felt as if I were surrounded by a constant whirling of incoming black clouds, and you'd survive one barrage of a storm only to see another coming in behind it."

Jadey looked around the pub and gestured to the stools at the bar. "Even this place was a symbol of my anger. Grandma didn't talk about Grandpa at all, really, except I remember her saying he was good at keeping a stool warm at Pete's Pub."

Jadey's voice lowered, her memories scratching old wounds.

"I've known a lot of really nice men in my life. I was just never related to any of them."

"I'm glad you at least had good friends here," Katie replied. "That must have counted for something."

"Oh, yeah, it definitely helped. I had a getaway. I had places to go where people would just hang out with each other, no undercurrents of anger. In our group, I was the angry one. The queen of pushing it down and letting it eat away at me. At least, that's the way I was until I hit twenty-three."

"What the hell happened at the age of twenty-three that took away your anger?"

Jadey stared at her beer, choosing her words. She shrugged.

"I became a writer. I mean I really focused on my writing. I channeled all of my stuff into words on a page, into stories, allowing my characters to act out things I never would have dreamed of really doing. I gave myself permission to express things I had never said out loud, and everything just flowed onto the page. For that I have my grandma to thank. She's the one who really showed me the importance of writing."

For a second, Jadey's thoughts returned to her grandma's journals and the mystery over where they were. But this was not the time to talk about it.

"Okay, I admit," she added, smiling. "I still think of myself as an angry person. At least sometimes. But I'm just not quite as riddled with it. Does that make sense?"

"Yes, and I'm happy for you. You found something you truly love to do, like me. Maybe 'The Jadey and Katie Show' was really a good name for us, because we ended up finding what really makes us happy."

Jadey, glad for the change of subject, turned her full attention to Katie. "You really do seem happy, Katie. Your salon is successful, you still have that same spunky personality which is what drew us all to you. Are you seeing anyone? Did going through a divorce ruin relationships for you?"

The question startled Katie at first. But then another long swallow of beer gave her some courage. She leaned in closer to talk just above a whisper in the crowded bar.

"Okay, you have to promise to keep this a secret because we can't let people know yet. I'm seeing Howard Dent, and when he can divorce his wife, we'll be able to be public about it."

Jadey sat stunned for a moment, panicked, not knowing what to say. She took a sip of beer to give her a second to collect her thoughts.

"You mean Chief Dent? As in the chief of police?"

"Yeah, isn't it funny? I mean, sure, he's about twenty years older than me, but there's something about him ... it makes me look forward to every time I see him. I know it looks bad because he's married, but she's a witch and they haven't been behaving like husband and wife, if you know what I mean, for years. I deserve to be happy, right?"

Katie's eyes gave away some apprehension, as if uncertain of the answer.

A glimmer of a memory hit Jadey. A flash in which she remembered scolding a young, teenage Katie for always going crazy over the jerks of the class. Her brain picked at a snippet of a conversation she recalled, telling Katie she was way too cute and cool to be hanging out with the guys who snuck around the back of the school to smoke, and whose wallets were stuffed with pictures ripped from *Playboy*.

Back to the present, she realized that Katie stared at her, waiting for a response.

"Yes, of course. You absolutely do. I'm sorry I looked so shocked. I suppose it's the age difference." Jadey searched in her heart for encouraging words. "Yes, you do deserve to be treated well. I wish the best for you."

"He's curious about you though," Katie said after another sip of beer. "He knows we're friends, so I suppose he thinks we've talked." Katie hesitated before probing with a question. "What are your plans, Jadey? Do you think you're back in Twin Station to stay?"

Jadey forced her face to show no reaction, but the hairs on her arms stood up. She managed a non-committal shrug. "I'm not sure yet. I've kind of stalled out on my remodeling plans, so let's see how that goes."

"Yes, let's see how it goes. Keep me updated on your plans."

Jadey managed a smile, but her mind reeled. How deeply was Katie involved in Dent's activities? And who else in town belonged to some conspiracy to make their neighbors disappear? Who exactly claimed that some didn't belong? She remembered Katie's snide remark about Jadey's gay friends, and shuddered.

She realized she needed to be very careful about saying anything about her experiences, because if Katie knew, Dent would know about it too. Could things get any more complicated?

Chapter 31

The raucous sound of a flock of geese overhead made Jadey look up, but she could barely see the formation as it disappeared into a dark cloud. The cacophony of honking continued, but slowly faded to silence. She looked down and realized she sat on the roof of the house and watched holes open up under her feet. Looking through the holes she noticed with interest she could see all the way into the cellar. The floors on the main level had collapsed, furniture plummeted into the chasm. Roofing material dropped down, and just kept falling forever.

The sun came through the living room curtains, which was her first clue she had fallen asleep on the couch. The odd position left a kink in her back, but she pulled herself up, stretched, and headed to the kitchen to start the coffee. Weirdo dream, she thought.

With the coffee brewing, Jadey headed up the stairs, but stopped on the third stair, the creaky one. She rocked it back and forth a few times, trying to identify exactly where the squeak came from. Just another thing she would have to tackle with her repairs. Would the tread need replacing, or could she just put in a couple of well-placed nails to firm it back down to the stringer? She looked at the rest of the staircase, picking out other signs of wear. After a minute, she decided the project would require better attention at another time, and she continued to the top of the stairs.

In her room, she pulled out a clean pair of jeans and an old, but clean t-shirt. With the fresh clothes and a pair of clean underwear, Jadey headed into the hall bathroom, eager to shake everything off with a hot shower. She wasn't hungover, but she felt out of sorts, her mind working its way back through the conversation she'd had with Katie the night before. She felt mostly confident, and she worried about her brain's haphazard insertion of the word "mostly," that Katie herself wasn't involved in any of the suspicious activity she'd been seeing. But her friend was close to someone whose actions worried her. Katie had always had an innocent, fun-loving personality. People were drawn to her because she was nice and probably a bit naïve. Unaware of the mesmerizing affect her early development had on the young men in school, Katie too often opened herself up to people whose intentions were unkind. Sweet Katie deserved to find someone who treated her well, but it didn't seem possible Howard Dent could be that person.

And the fact he was married gave Jadey kind of a sick feeling. Her hand reached subconsciously to her stomach. Did those thoughts make her sick, or WAS she actually hungover? Mostly she was just confused.

By the time she dried herself, Jadey determined to pick up the search for Grandma Ellie's journals. Maybe all her questions would be answered there, but even if not, the fact she couldn't find them made her all the more eager to look.

Back on the main floor, coffee cup in hand, she thought about how she had to tackle this. She had covered just about everything inside the house. Even the creepy cellar had yielded nothing except for cobwebs in her hair. She stared out the window and realized she hadn't even considered the outside of the house. The property never had a garage, so the possibilities were limited. But Grandma's zeal for gardening gave Jadey hope the outdoors may have proved an intriguing prospect for the older woman's hiding places.

She thought about the shed. An obvious spot, but she cringed at having to tackle such a mess. Pushing open the back door of the house, Jadey stood for a moment and stared at the old outbuilding. Once she yanked the door open, she glared at the jumble of rakes and hoes and shovels and stacks of old pots. Every wall had hooks from which hung clippers and saws for cutting small tree limbs. Every corner was wedged full of fertilizer containers, garden gloves, and bags of bulbs, waiting to be planted in the fall.

She sighed as she gazed at the jungle, and then began the process of taking everything out, one at a time. As long as you're going to do this, take the opportunity to organize it, she told herself. Everything she took out went into one stack or another. She placed the big tools, the shovels and rakes, off to one side, and, in a separate pile, some of the older, rustier duplicates. In her head, she planned for those to go to the metals recycling center.

Jadey placed planter pots together in another part of the yard, organized by size. Broken ones went into a separate stack to go in the trash.

The myriad of smaller tools had their own places too, and whenever she saw a duplicate, she took the oldest looking one and put it with other tools headed to the metals recycler.

The process wasn't as bad as she thought it would be, and she could see from her piles that when she put everything back in an orderly fashion, the shed might actually have room to spare.

As she got down to the last of the odds and ends, she started examining the walls. None of the pots held anything interesting, and she hadn't found any other kind of container to hold the journals, so the next move was to think like Grandma Ellie. A woman who could turn half of her closet into a safe room would probably hide something important in another secret compartment, although this one would surely be much smaller. A couple of built-in shelves in the shed gave her hope for a possible key to the puzzle, but none of them provided any hiding place for notebooks. The back wall was solid, although it didn't fit quite as tightly to the neighboring walls as the rest of the shed, and she figured the winters caused the ground to shift a bit, throwing the shed out of level.

She knocked on the ceiling and the floor, and felt around the door frame to see if anything moved. Eventually she had to admit that nothing came close to looking like a hiding place in the shed. Jadey groaned at the job of putting everything back ahead of her. Stepping out of the shed, her eye caught on an odd anomaly in the door.

The top half of the wooden door was thicker than the bottom half, built-up as if extra wood had been nailed on. Large hooks across the top had held several digging tools that now lay in the piles outside, but now she noticed a smaller hook, turned sideways, on the heftier part of the door.

Jadey smiled, proud of her grandma's workmanship. She hadn't notice this before, and neither would anyone else, but having found the safe room in the closet upstairs, she recognized the same little hook here. Almost afraid to try it, Jadey slipped her finger inside the loop of the hook, took a breath, and turned it.

Just like the door to the safe room, this gave a little click as the quarter turn released its hold. The panel now swung open with the help of two small hinges on the inside. Tucked in tightly, three green notebooks peeked over the top of a plywood rail.

Chapter 32

Her legs couldn't carry her fast enough through the door and into the house. Leaving all the tools and garden implements where she sorted them on the ground, she hugged the notebooks tightly to her, as if they would disappear as quickly as they had just appeared to her. She headed to the living room and carefully spread them out on the small coffee table in front of the couch.

The books felt like precious gems to Jadey. Like she had uncovered a buried treasure and these worn, tattered notebooks were the find of the century. She opened the first one and looked at the date of the initial entry, noting that it was February 23, 2016, the day after the last entry on the journals she had found in Grandma's bedroom. A quick peek at the last date of the third notebook, made her throat catch. It was May 1, 2020, the day before she died. Jadey could imagine her writing in these secret journals and then immediately hiding them in the shed, afraid to leave any of them lying around for others to find.

She began to read, fascinated by the content, but also marveling once again at her grandma's ability to relay events and draw the reader in as if she had written a mystery novel. She gave names, and dates, and specifics about conversations with the people who felt harassed or threatened, and the friends like Lily Sheridan who offered her own pieces of information. Some of Grandma's entries were speculation and her own observations, but much of it contained testimony from people in the community whose information she trusted. Jadey kept turning page after page, absorbing all she could learn.

An hour later her stomach reminded her she had skipped breakfast, so Jadey headed to the makeshift kitchen to see what was left of the cereal. The box was nearly empty, but she figured she could make it work. She opened the refrigerator and peered into the carton of milk. What was in the bottom, about six tablespoons? She rummaged around a bit but besides a box of crackers, not much of anything edible magically appeared before her. She glanced back at the notebooks in the other room, eager to get back to them, but her stomach yelled at her to put something in it. A trip to the grocery store might have to bump the notebooks back for a half hour.

As she returned the cereal box to the temporary counter, her eye caught something in the insulation between the studs on the wall by the back door. Tilting a little closer, she realized she saw what appeared to be a very small lens. Had the builder dropped something when the house was built and covered it with drywall years ago?

No, this looked very new, and she would have noticed it when she demoed the wall recently. She used her fingers to push aside the insulation covering most of it, and examined the object. Oh my god, a tiny camera. Stunned, she pulled it out and fingered the small battery pack with a thin antenna wire snaking from it. She felt a strangled cry move up her throat. What the hell was going on? She turned the camera around in her hands, being careful now not to have it pointed at her face. Was someone spying on her. Why? Who would do this? Who would be able to get into her house?

Then she remembered coming home from her visit with her mom and having the sensation someone was in the house. She had had a gut feeling someone who didn't belong had stirred the air. Tears blurred her eyesight as she scrambled with the back of the camera, desperately pulling on the back panel to gain access to the battery. It needed a screwdriver, a tiny Phillips-head, so she turned to where her tool box sat on the far side of the kitchen.

After removing the back panel, she held the tiny battery in her hand and set the camera on the floor, planning to stomp on it and destroy it. But after a second, she thought better of it. The thing was disabled now, and maybe she would need it as proof of her fears, although she had no idea who to approach with it. She couldn't go to the police. Her gut told her the chief of police had something to do with this. She couldn't tell Katie because of her relationship with Dent. She wouldn't tell her mom because her mom would worry about her.

She would call Doug. He could help. He could give her advice. He would help her make some sense of this.

Chapter 33

By the time Doug arrived, Jadey found two more cameras. The one in her bedroom almost made her throw up as she thought about the invasion of her privacy. She also found one in her grandma's bedroom. As Doug came into the house, she held them out to him, the tiny batteries in one hand and the three small cameras in the other.

Doug looked at her hands, and then her face, confused. "I got the donuts you asked for. What's up with those?"

"Thanks. I'm starving. I had to talk to someone. I found these hidden here, in my house." Her voice grew louder. "Who would have put hidden cameras in my house?" She was both angry and confused. Doug's face was white, and he shook his head, sharing her confusion.

"Cameras?" He picked one up and turned it in his hand as if he'd find the answers written on the camera itself. "Jadey, this is creepy. Where did you find these?"

"The first one was right there." She pointed to the spot between the studs where she pulled out some insulation to get to it. "It had to have been planted recently because it wasn't there when I tore down the wall."

"Who else has been in the house? Who would have had access?"

Jadey set the cameras down and paced. "No one, really. Mrs. Sheridan from next door was here, and Sergeant Dillanian stopped in the same day." She froze, thinking about him. Dillanian worked for Dent. Who the hell was in on this thing?

"Doug, what is happening in this town? I've had conversations with people and have seen some things, and I'm starting to think that behind the rooster-motif curtains there's something almost evil going on in this town. What happened to Twin Station?"

"Honest, Jadey, I don't know about anything that would have led to someone putting spy gadgets in your house. This is crazy. But you're right, Twin Station isn't exactly Mayberry, if you know what I mean. People here have gotten kind of, I don't know, protective? A lot of people are afraid people are trying to change things, to take away our town."

"What are you talking about? Who's taking the town?"

Doug turned away, unable to look into Jadey's eyes.

"You have to understand. These are good people who work hard all the time, and they see others who just want what they have. Not everyone works for it. Some people are just takers."

Jadey stared at him. The room became still. Doug felt the tension in the air and tried to break it by holding up the bag in his hand.

"Donuts?"

Jadey yanked the bag from him. "You're damn right. Donuts." She jammed her hand into the bag and pulled out a chocolate glazed old-fashioned donut. Her face softened. She looked at Doug.

"You remembered. My favorite kind."

He smiled and shrugged, not sure exactly where they were on the scale of heated argument versus old time remembrances.

For the next minute, neither spoke. Jadey bit into the donut and wandered to the window overlooking the backyard. Her eyes caught on the shed that just became her secret treasure chest. She chewed on the donut while Doug, his own donut leaving white powdered sugar on his shirt, joined her.

"What's with all of the tools spread out over the yard?"

Jadey felt her breath catch. She tried for nonchalance in her voice.

"I'm just organizing. Things were so jammed in there you couldn't find anything." Her eyes subconsciously darted back to the other room where the notebooks still sat on the coffee table. Why didn't she tuck them away somewhere? She needed to hide them. She had to make sure Doug didn't go into the other room.

"Doug, when you talk about people coming to take things, are you talking about diverse ethnicities? Like me?"

"What? No! People like you? Jadey, you're one of us. You were born here."

"But I'm bi-racial, and I can't help but notice that Twin Station is about as white as a marshmallow. Am I scary?"

"No, of course not." Doug was adamant. "You're ... I mean ... I don't know if anyone ever thought of you as, you know, Black, or anything." Doug's neck felt hot, his discomfort growing. Jadey stared at him, letting the unease hang in the air.

"It's different when you've known someone since they were a kid." Doug tried to explain. "We first met in kindergarten, goddammit. I'm talking about those others, who move in here where they've got no stakes, no history. They're not like us. You know what I mean, don't you?"

"I do know what you mean, Doug, and Twin Station isn't the first town to feel that way. But think about this. You don't put me in the same category because you know me. You and others aren't afraid of me because they have gone to school with me, taught me, sold me groceries, spent time in conversations with me. Isn't that the whole point? We fear what we don't know, but if we take the time to get to know people, we stop thinking of them as 'others.' Don't we?"

Doug shrugged. Silent. Jadey stared at him.

"It's like a giant neon sign pointing out how we fear people because we have some kind of preconceived idea of who they are. What they represent. And when we actually take some time to get to know them, we find out they're really all just like you. People with different colored skin still want the same things you do – to raise a family, to earn a decent wage, to belong to a church, or a neighborhood, to go to a baseball game, or a carnival. How is that so different than everyone else in this town?"

Doug shook his head. "I hear you Jadey, but you can't change something people have been believing for generations. And I understand many of their fears, I do. But I also see what you're saying."

Jadey pointed to the three cameras on the table. "Look what it's come to! Look at what people will do to stay in their little bubbles. Someone had to break into my house and threaten me. You think that's normal? You think that's okay so they can keep their kids safe from the bogeyman they made up?"

"No, I don't think that's okay." He looked at the cameras and turned to Jadey. "I think you might be in danger, Jadey. I hate to say it, but I think you should leave. Now. I don't want to say much about it, but some crazy shit is about to happen, and I can't stop it, and I would just die if you got hurt."

Chapter 34

onnors approached Chief Dent's office with his hat in his hand. He stood quietly, looking around at the walls of the office he had seen a thousand times while he waited for Dent to look up from his paperwork and acknowledge him.

"Whattya got?" Dent snapped, irritated at the interruption.

"She found the cameras. Three of 'em anyway. The fourth one's still active."

Dent stared at him, saying nothing. The color rising above his shirt collar was the only indication of his slow burn.

"But there's other news. She found the notebooks too. Before she started pulling out the cameras, I caught a good view of her coming in the back door with three notebooks in her hand, and she sat right down on the couch and started flipping through them."

Dent stood, grunting with the effort. "So, it was true. The Evans bitch was keeping notes."

Connors stood as still as he could make himself.

"She's had time to read them." Dent stared at Connors. "Do we know if she's talked to anyone?"

"Can't tell. The only functioning camera is in the living room. She cleared out the cameras in her own room and the old lady's and the one in the kitchen."

"So, she knows someone is watching, but maybe doesn't know who yet. She's going to have a heightened sense of urgency, but we don't know what she's going to do. We have to act before she has a chance, and the timing couldn't be worse because you know what's happening this weekend."

Connors nodded, happy to not have to actually speak.

Dent made up his mind and waved to dismiss Connors. "I'll do this. Go back to work. I'm going to take care of her."

Chapter 35

Jadey stretched to loosen the cramps from sitting so long while she pored over the last of the three journals. Things were starting to make sense now. Pieces of information fell into place to explain events. The pages described Ellie's gradual realization that, for a couple of decades, some of the elements in town had been engaging in a systematic terrorizing of people who didn't fit into their prejudicial concept of who belonged and who didn't. Quite different from Ellie Evans' earlier journals, which had reminisced about fun trips with her granddaughter and bridge games with her friends, these three focused on rumors about abusive behavior in the police department, and secret meetings among some of the townspeople.

Some of the notes in the journals contained speculation, but her grandmother's documentation included information about people who suddenly left, or houses suddenly placed for sale, even after the family just made commitments to participate in town events, or had just set up a business. They were strange, confusing happenings, until Grandma Ellie started to list them, and group them, and show the patterns.

And within the pages of these three notebooks, Ellie Evans made a list of people she hid in her home, and, in times of danger, in her safe room, until they could gather their things safely and move out of town.

The whole scenario sent chills through Jadey. This was evidence of an intentional course of racism and terror, seemingly taking over her hometown. Was it always that way, and she never saw it as a child? Or did it start more recently, the result of some event or personality that took the reins and began to quietly attract others with the same bigoted mindset?

The story of Joe's disappearance made much more sense now because Joe would have been a perceived danger to their idea of sameness and harmony. Grandma's journals made some things crystal clear and provided her with news for her mom. She looked at her watch. Her mom would still be at work. She'd wait until the end of the workday so she and her mom could talk without interruption.

As Jadey looked out the back window, she remembered all the tools she left lying in the yard. Her mind drifted back to what Doug told her this morning. Some crazy shit is about to happen. Could it really get any crazier? Did it have something to do with the cameras she found? Somehow, she must have backed into something, and all the questions about whether she would stay, the feelings of someone watching her, or breaking into her house, the horrible implication her grandma may have been murdered for what she knew....

Doug was probably right; she should get out of there. But her stubborn side didn't want to run away and just allow this to continue. Who else is getting hurt? She worried about Katie and her relationship with Dent. Dent. Jadey felt in her gut that the chief of police was involved in all of this. Whatever "this" was. She couldn't just pack up her clothes and leave, could she? This was once her home. This had once been her town.

Deciding to get outside and put her mind on something else for a while, she headed for the shed and the mass of tools lying in the grass. Jadey picked up a couple of the shovels she planned to keep and stepped back into the shed. Before hanging them, she glanced down, again noticing the gap between the back wall and the floor. How odd she wasn't seeing grass through the small space. If the ground had settled and caused the small building to shift and become uneven, that gap should have been an opening to the outside.

Curious, she stepped through the door and walked around to the back of the shed, looking for the gap from the exterior of the small structure. It hit her. She again felt that sensation, the prickle on the nape of her neck, the queasy drop in her stomach, the familiar "Oh shit."

From the outside, the dimensions of the shed were clearly bigger than they were on the inside. Had her wiley grandma built yet another false wall and created a third secret space? What the hell was hidden now? For the moment, she forgot the fear and worries about a prowler, possible murder, bigoted neighbors that might want to see her harmed. Was there another hook that would unlock this secret space?

A quick survey of the exterior showed no signs of a means of entry, so access had to come from inside the shed. But once back in, it became quickly clear; this would not open easily. She found no magic hook, but she could see dozens of large nails that attached the back to the side walls, with others toenailed into the floor and ceiling. Someone who did not want this wall opened, nailed it in by hand. And used an entire box of nails to do it.

She looked at the tools splayed out on the lawn and spotted a couple of crowbars. With a feeling of both excitement and dread, she returned to the shed and wedged the curved edge of the largest crowbar into the small gap that originally caught her attention.

She found, after some trial and error, that if she rocked the crowbar back and forth, she could get the wall to move a bit, and then, when it settled back into place, a nail head was left protruding a fraction. The smaller crowbar worked well to pull that nail out, although it came reluctantly, as if the years had caused the wood to grow around it. She slid the bigger crowbar back into the opening that, because of her work, was now a tiny bit bigger. Little by little she extended the size of the opening by rocking the wood and then levering an exposed nail out. One at a time. She talked to herself. One at a time.

Sweat dripped into her eyes. The day was hot to begin with, and being in this small shed where the only opening was the single door, made the inside stifling. She could go in the house and grab a fan, but she didn't know if she had an extension cord long enough to bring it this far into the yard, and besides, she didn't want to stop her progress.

Now it felt urgent. She had to see what grandma hid in the back of the shed.

After about a half hour of sweat and muscles, she freed up one side of the false wall. One down, three to go. She pulled up the hem of her shirt and wiped her forehead and paused to stare at her progress. Hoping the second step would be a bit easier, she set back to work. The nails across the top had been toenailed into the ceiling, which meant they left a bigger part of the head for her pry tools to grab onto and pull out. She couldn't shake the bewilderment, flabbergasted her grandma had held so many secrets, and for so many years. Clearly this wood panel had been in place here for a long time. Each long nail made a drawn-out groaning sound, as if extremely reluctant to be removed from the wood it held together.

When the top of the wall was free, she forgot the heat and the sweat and her thirst and aching back. She was rabid in her determination to get that wall out of there and went to work on the bottom, where the panel met the floor. She mouthed invectives against her grandma for her overuse of nails. For god's sake, you could have put this wall in with half the number of nails! What was so important that made you spend an entire day hammering?

At last she pulled the final nail from the bottom, which meant only the left side of the panel was still nailed in.

Jadey stood up, grabbed her back which threatened to lock-up on her, and looked at the three unsecured sides. A look at the remaining nails assured her no handy set of hinges would help her this time. She used her sleeve to wipe sweat out of her eyes and then put her hand in the small space where her quest had begun. Could she pull hard enough to just rip the rest of it open by bending back the wall? Would the nails give on their own with the torque she could create?

She found some give. The wall moved enough that now she got both hands in the opening and could feel the old wood yielding. She ignored the screams from her back and arms as she pulled hard. Within minutes she had enough of the wall moved that she could gain some leverage and really put pressure on the wood and shift it from the place it had been nailed for years. Jadey pulled the panel far enough so that she could look into the opening, and shrieked at the face looking back at her.

Chapter 36

Dillanian pushed the gas pedal to get ahead of the light traffic, and then pulled a quick right, turning into a long driveway next to a boarded-up brick-faced building. The stacked-stone retaining wall that separated the driveway from the neglected hillside of the neighboring property threatened to topple as the soil slowly pushed back at the brave attempt to contain it. He angled his car around to the back of the warehouse, where empty loading docks and shuttered windows reflected the disappearing manufacturing focus in this part of the country. Weeds grew up between the cracks in the asphalt surface, and the parking lot gathered paper and other trash the wind whirled in. The back lot was hidden from the main street so it was his favorite place to talk on the phone without interruption.

The number he called was direct to an office sixty miles away and staffed 24/7. The gravelly voice on the other end sounded impatient and hurried.

"Dade."

"It's Dillanian. It's a go."

"I'm pulling the file. Is anyone with you?"

Dillanian sighed. "Dade, how long have I been doing this?"

"Sorry. Never mind. Whattya got?"

Dillanian tapped his fingers on the steering wheel, agitated and rushed. "We're at forty-eight hours, and it's ..."

"Fucking what? Forty-eight hours? What happened to push it up?"

"I can't tell, everything's really tight here. The ammo is ready to be shipped and the guns are going separately. It looks like as many as fifteen more cars are coming in, so it's going to be a full caravan."

"Shit, Dillanian. We haven't even nailed down the target yet. I can't send enough forces to three different places on spec!"

"I know. I have something in mind that may mean we don't have to know the targets. Let me check out a couple of things and I'll get back."

"Make it fast. I want your back completely covered."

"Funny. That's what I want too."

Chapter 37

Jadey's reflexive response to finding a face staring at her was to jerk back so fast she almost fell out of the shed's open door. Fighting the urge to run, she took an extra second to breathe, and then dared to look again at what had frightened her. The person staring at her hadn't moved, and the darkness of the shed hid the details she strained to see.

Oh my god, it's a skeleton. Or is it? Jadey stared at the thing behind the wall. In spite of the bad lighting in the shed, she soon began to make out features. She swore under her breath and then crept close again. Sure enough, a skull, with empty eye sockets looked right at her, as if to mirror her actions and study her too. Thin leathery skin covered the skull, and a few tufts of brown hair stuck to places where the skin clung on top. "A mummy," she whispered.

A tattered plaid shirt covered most of the torso of the skeleton. Time had faded the colors, and the threads were thinned, showing, she guessed, perhaps decades of time in the dark, hidden compartment. Below the waist the remains of some denim pants hung listlessly, snagged on a jutting hip bone, on a body that no longer filled out the dimensions of the pants.

Her brain, now calmed a bit as she surveyed the sight in front of her, tried to process what she saw. What the hell was a mummy doing in the back of Grandma Ellie's shed? And hidden behind a fake wall? Did Grandma do this, or has this been here longer than the family owned the house?

The body was in a semi-standing position, pinned against the back of the shed. Clearly the fake wall held it up all these years, and now it seemed kind of fused into place. The blank eyes creeped her out, and she moved her attention to where the tattered boots met the floor. There, next to the boots, was a gun. Jadey knew a little about guns, and she recognized a revolver. A very old revolver. Her eyes shot back up to the skull and for the first time she saw a clean hole in the center of the forehead.

Okay, she thought to herself. Think. Think. Someone was murdered here, but it was a long time ago. It's a man, she figured, based on the clothes. What should I do? I know I should probably call the police, but oh man, I really don't want anything to do with Chief Dent. He'd probably try to pin this on me. She laughed, realizing her thoughts were bouncing between rational and irrational. Should I try to get a hold of Greg Dillanian? Can I trust him? What the hell happened here so long ago?

And suddenly, understanding hit her like a brick. She knew who it was. Or she thought she did. She moved a little closer, trying to get a good look at the denim pants that hung from the mummified remains. One of the back pockets sagged with weight. An outline of a bulky form caught her eye. Was it possible a wallet was left with the skeleton? Finding an ID would be fascinating.

Jadey ran outside the shed and picked up a small hoe. Back in the shed, she again approached the man, the mummy, whatever he was now, and extended the hoe to the pants, trying to catch them so she could reach the back pocket without having to touch anything. The long tool helped her attempts to reach around the pants, but her hands were sweaty and her brain rapidly fired through scenarios of terror. Eventually she managed to pull the back of the fabric around and toward her, and then, carefully, she slid her thumb and index finger into the pocket. She cringed just touching the rotting fabric and pulled her fingers back out quickly.

All right, Jadey, you can do this. Whoever this was is long dead. Just reach in and grab whatever is in that pocket. Don't smell, and don't think. Don't look at the skeleton. Don't look at the face. Oh god, this was horrible. That leathery skin, that hole in the middle of its forehead. Just focus. Get the wallet. You have to see if you're right.

Once again, her fingers dipped into the back pocket. It felt like a wallet. Get a grip girl, she thought, and then laughed out loud at her unintentional joke. Yes, get a grip on that thing, whatever it is. Her heart pounding, she finally got enough of a grasp and began to carefully work it up and out of the back pocket.

She dropped the hoe with disgust. It had touched those pants, hanging from the mummy. She stared at the wallet in her hands. The leather was stiff from years of disuse and exposure to extreme elements. She thought about the weather. This skeleton would have been assaulted with the cold of below-zero winters, and the heat of ninety-degree summer days. Humidity, dryness – if this had been there as long as she surmised, the skeleton would have endured the wrath of many seasons.

With the wallet in her hands, she hesitated for a moment. What secrets did it hold? How many more surprises could her heart take? She finally worked the hardened leather open and peered at the old driver's license in the grainy plastic window. It confirmed what she had guessed. "Hello Grandpa," she said aloud. "So, this is where you've been."

Chapter 38

Jadey walked back and forth across the floor of the gutted kitchen, hearing the ring on the other end, praying her mother would answer. On the fourth ring, a breathless Trish apologized.

"Sorry Jadey. Hi. I was out in back watering flowers when I heard my phone. I have to tell you about how great the dahlias look this year."

"Mom, wait. I'm calling about something important. Are you sitting down?"

"Oh, god, Jadey. What happened? Are you okay? Have you been in an accident?"

"Mom, I'm fine. I found out a couple of things. Some really important things. It can't wait until I can see you in person." She took a deep breath, still rattled. "The first thing is ... oh geez, I don't know what to tell you first. I think I know what happened to Joe."

"Joe? What are you talking about? Where is Joe?"

"I found your mom's old journals. She had hidden them in the shed. I'll tell you all about that later."

"The shed? She hid her journals in the shed? What do you mean?"

"Mom. Listen. This is important. Grandma had been keeping track of some terrible things happening here in Twin Station. Going way back. Even back to the time we were still living here. She was taking notes about families who were leaving suddenly, like they were being forced out of town, and of Black and Asian men who were just disappearing."

"Okay," Trish said with the sound of a chair scraping the floor in the background. "I'm sitting. What are you talking about?"

"I'll let you read this all for yourself, but the bottom line is, Grandma uncovered a conspiracy of some kind aimed at ridding Twin Station of people of color, going back decades. Your mom, and a few others, had some kind of theory about the police department orchestrating this crazy thing. I don't know what you'd call it. Ethnic cleansing? It was like a small-town white supremacist group, or Klan, or something, and when new families of color moved in, the group did underhanded things to try to get them to leave."

"You mean like burn crosses on their lawns? I don't remember anything like that."

"No, much more subtle. Quiet, anonymous threats. Little things happening, like broken door locks, gas poured on their floors, dead animal parts arriving in their mail. And the worst is there were several Black men who simply disappeared. Left in the morning for work and never came back. It happened to Grandma's friends Harold and Sonya. He just disappeared while out running an errand. She called the police, but they were no help and actually told her he probably just wanted to start a new life somewhere else."

"My mom had all this in her journals?"

"Yes, she was keeping track. Logging all of the information because she was trying to figure it all out. But she couldn't go to anyone with it because it was becoming apparent it was the police who were in on it. At least some of them. One of the ones back in those days is now the Chief of Police, so she couldn't trust anyone."

"My mom was doing all that? Investigating? I can't even picture her ..."

"Even more, Mom. She was hiding some of them. There are notes in her journals about people she actually hid in a safe room until they could pull their things together and get out of town."

"Seriously?" Trish couldn't hide the shock in her voice. "It's hard to take all of this in. I don't know what to think." Neither spoke for a minute.

"What were you saying about Joe? Was he one of the ones ...?" Trish couldn't bear to finish the question.

Jadey hesitated, her voice now changing from urgency to compassion.

"That's what Grandma figured out – years after that day he rode off on his bike and never came back. She thinks he was one of the ones the police made disappear, which means she thinks they killed him. The idea of a Black man impregnating a White girl was beyond what they could stand. I think they killed him, Mom. I think those bastards killed Joe."

A long silence followed. Jadey wondered if they had been disconnected.

"Are you okay, Mom? I know this sounds crazy, but even in the short time I've been back I've seen some stuff."

"Jadey, you need to get out of there. You need to leave. If this is all true, you're in danger because you're the daughter of a Black man. You're half Black. They're going to hurt you."

"Mom, it's okay. I'm okay. I've already decided, now that I've read this stuff, I'm not going to stay here, so I'll be back soon."

"No, right now! Get out. Just leave. What if they've decided you're not 'one of them' like the crazy assholes they are? What if they decide they need you to disappear too?"

"Don't worry. I've got friends here. I'm perfectly safe. You know how tough I am."

"What friends? Who are you sure you can trust? How do you know who is doing these things?"

Jadey didn't have an answer, and it troubled her. Who could she trust? Even her old best friend, Katie, was tied up in an affair with the man that Jadey was sure led the entire ugly thing. She changed subjects.

"There's something else, Mom. You're not going to believe this, but I found Grandpa."

Jadey heard an audible gasp on the other end of the line. Then silence.

"I found Grandpa, Mom. He's been in the shed all along."

"What are you talking about? Jadey, what ...?"

"Mom, listen. All of these years you've been so angry at Grandma for not believing you? Not protecting you? She did it, Mom. She did it. She believed you and she made sure Grandpa would never hurt you again. She shot him all those years ago and hid his body in the back of the shed and then put up a wall so no one would find him."

Again, silence on the other end.

"Mom, your mom risked it all to save you. She killed the man who molested you."

"Why didn't she tell me? Why did she let me believe she didn't care?"

"The only thing I can think of is she didn't dare tell a twelve-year-old. What if you accidentally let it leak? They could have arrested her, and then you would have had no one. Or maybe she worried you'd hate her for being the kind of person who could kill her own husband. And it would have put such a big burden on you. I'm sure she thought it was safer to just make up the story that he left on his own."

"Oh my god, this is .... " Jadey heard a little giggle on the other end of the phone, and then her mom burst into full-fledged laughter.

"I know this is so inappropriate, to laugh like this." Her mother gasped into the phone. "It's just so absurd, but also so damned perfect." Trish howled with laughter on the other end.

Jadey found herself smiling at her own mom's reaction. "Mom, you know you're laughing about someone else's murder, right?"

Trish sighed, the laughter subsiding. "I know. But they can't put me in jail for laughing. It's just the picture I have in my head, all the time hating him for leaving us, but glad he was gone – and it turned out he was in the shed all along. Good god, she stuffed him in the shed!"

More laughter.

"He was a big guy. Jadey, my god, how do you think she did it?"

"One thing I've learned about Grandma Ellie is when she really needed to, she could do just about anything. I love knowing she ultimately protected you. That's the Grandma I thought I knew all these years."

"Wow. We've got more to talk about, I guess, when you get home. I want to know all about how you found him, but right now I have a lot to think about. Poor Joe. That explanation makes much more sense because I always knew he would never leave me voluntarily, but I can't stand what they did to him. We've got to turn over Grandma's notes to some police agency. The federal marshals, or state police or whoever. I can't even think straight."

"We will, Mom. I'm keeping them safe and we'll figure out who needs to know so we can finally get justice for Joe, and all of the others they hurt."

"You have to come home, Baby. Come home right now."

"I'll be there soon. I'm all right. Give me another day or two and I'll figure out what to do with the house and everything. I don't think I'll be making Twinktown my home again."

Chapter 39

Jadey paced the room and noticed her hands shaking. Her conversation with her mom earlier in the day forced her to think about things in a more methodical way. She admonished herself to take time to deal with the emotions later, because right now she had to think about things clearly and logically. But she couldn't calm the rapid-fire thoughts that left her anxious.

Still wearing the cargo pants and t-shirt she put on that morning, she curled up on her grandma's bed. That morning. It seemed like a lifetime ago. She laid the journals in front of her and picked up the most recent one. Passages in the notebooks answered some of the questions Jadey had, but brought up many more. She focused on Ellie Evans' passages about hiding some people in her safe room. One involved a woman from South Korea who moved to Twin Station from Boston, where she originally settled as an immigrant. Living alone, the woman found herself the target of harassment, most of it through anonymous mail and hang-up phone calls, but at one point felt so threatened, she sought safety at Ellie's house. When the police knocked on her door late at night, Ellie hid the terrified woman in her safe room.

From what Jadey could guess, Grandma Ellie originally constructed the room about three years before, after another neighbor sought refuge with her. The pattern became clear: people of color were made to feel uncomfortable, unwelcome and eventually fearful. Some of the men disappeared altogether. Women sought shelter, and then quietly moved away.

A single lamp lit the bedroom, and Jadey kept glancing at the window, listening to an owl in the distance. The night was dark, with the sliver of a moon hidden behind clouds. Very few of the lights from town reached the wider spaces where this house stood, and glimpsing outside felt like looking into a black hole. She stretched, and got up to turn on more lights, hoping to wash away the sense of danger and doom creeping up on her.

As soon as she stood to get to the light switch on the wall, she heard a faint sound of a click from downstairs. Jadey froze in place and listened. Carefully she reached over and turned off the lamp by the bed, and then stood silently, listening for more sounds.

Another sound, very faint. The back of Jadey's neck chilled with fear. Was she imagining it? Was it just wind up against the old house? With as little movement as she could manage, she reached onto the bed and scooped up the three notebooks. Now the noises downstairs became more pronounced, as if whoever was inside the house didn't care if she knew it. Or maybe he thought she wasn't there and walked around carelessly. The sounds of footsteps indicated the person walked from room to room downstairs.

Jadey crept quietly toward her grandma's closet. The safe room. I have to get to the safe room. Worried she might step on a creaky floorboard she tried to do slide motions, angry at herself for not having paid attention to which floorboards creaked in the room. She reached the closet door just as she heard the footsteps come closer to the bottom of the stairway. She almost screamed when a voice suddenly called out in a kind of sing-songy way, taunting her from downstairs.

"Jadey. Jaaaadey. I know you're here. Come on down and let's talk."

That voice. She knew it, she thought, but the way who-ever it was kind of sang out her name confused her. Is it Doug? Did he plant those cameras after all? The voice was a man's, and definitely one who knew her. Dillanian? She was terrified she couldn't identify the voice for sure. Now in the back of the closet, she reached for the hook to open the secret door.

The footsteps started up the stairs and she almost cried out when she heard the distinctive creak on the third step. The intruder paused to listen.

Jadey managed to turn the hook enough for the secret door to swing in. Thank God for well-oiled hinges. As quietly as she could, she straightened the clothes on the hanger before she closed the door, hoping to cover any sign she had come through here. Once inside the safe room, she quietly closed and latched the door from the inside, and stood perfectly still, listening.

The intruder started up the stairs again, not afraid of telegraphing his ascent. Jadey felt around the pitch-black room and reached out for the old cushion on the floor. She tugged the notebooks to her chest and lowered herself, careful not to make a sound. Aware that even her own inhaling and exhaling made a small noise, she pulled her sleeve up in front of her mouth.

The footsteps reached the top of the stairs and turned, heading down the hall toward where her room was, and her mom's at the end of the hall. How fortunate she had chosen to sit in her grandma's room tonight while she sorted through the notebooks.

Some time passed. Without any light in the cramped space her eyes had nothing to adjust to, but she didn't dare try one of the flashlights. Occasional sounds of a closet door opening and things being moved around broke the silence. Then more footsteps, in the distance, heading further down the hall toward her mother's room. Again, a door opened, more sounds, more footsteps, until they suddenly became louder as the intruder headed back in the direction of the room at the top of the stairs where she sheltered. She could make out what sounded like a quick check of the hall bathroom, and then the footsteps unbearably close, as the prowler stepped into her grandma's bedroom.

A pause. No sounds. She could imagine him looking around, scoping out the room. No doubt his eyes were accustomed to the dark with light from the early moon shining in. She suspected he sought out any movement and strained his ears to listen for any sounds. And then the voice again, but this time with menace.

"Jadey. It's over. Come on out. I just want those journals. No one is going to hurt you."

Dent. The voice was much clearer now. He no longer tried to disguise it, and he injected his characteristic authoritative intensity as he demanded she show herself. Jadey breathed as softly as she could, holding her position on the cushion, not moving a muscle. She heard him resume his search in the room just outside the closet, and then eventually heard his heavy footsteps step inside the closet itself. The distinctive sound of the bulb being lit as he pulled the dangling string startled her. She fought the urge to cry out. He was two feet from her, in a fully lit closet, and her only hope was that grandma's construction on the safe room door would fool him.

How many times had this happened before that someone, maybe even her grandma, hid in this room, holding their breath, praying not to be found? At least until this point the hidden room must have held its secrets, because if Dent knew of it, he would be pushing the door open right now.

She felt herself queasy with fear. As she sat in the total darkness, she felt her stomach flip over and sweat pop out on her forehead. Oh god, was she going to throw up? So far, she had managed to remain completely quiet, but ... Oh no, her fear was making her light headed, and she thought she might lose her dinner, right there. Her hand reached out, feeling for the bucket. She continued to breathe through the fabric of her shirt.

He stood still. She could hear his inhaling and exhaling, and his breathing sounded angry and labored. For a minute or two she heard no sounds on his side of the door, and Jadey felt certain he had to know only the wall separated them. He was just waiting her out. She had nowhere to go but right into his grasp. Should she take an offensive stance? Maybe surprise him by opening the door and running out? Could she catch him off balance and get far enough away from him while he took a second to figure out what happened? If he was going to catch her, at least she wanted to make it as hard on him as she could.

Relieved, she eventually heard the sound of his boots turn on the wooden floor and leave the closet. But he wasn't done. She heard more sounds, imagining him on the floor, looking under the bed and then pulling the half-finished afghan out of the basket in the corner. His movements sounded angry, punishing. Moments later, the heavy thump of his shoes told her he left the room, and then she heard him quickly head down the stairs.

Only then did Jadey recognize the throb of her heart, pounding out a cadence in her head. If Dent had heard what she was hearing in her ears, it would have alerted him to her hiding spot. She was still aware of him, because now he moved noisily around downstairs, unconcerned about the sounds he made. She pictured his large mass as he paced the lower level. Was he turning over furniture, opening doors? The noises sounded as if he stopped in the former kitchen. Was he looking for the cameras?

What was he doing? She was sure he was still there, but just quieter now. After another couple of minutes, she heard the back door close and pictured him walking away. But she worried he might be faking it. Was he pretending to leave, figuring he'd catch her when she came out of hiding? He didn't know where she was, but he was probably pretty sure she was in the house if he had seen the lamp on in her grandma's bedroom just before he came inside.

She didn't dare chance it. If she had to, she'd sleep in the safe room, as she imagined others had before her. Her stomach quieted now. The immediate threat was over. She repositioned herself for a long stay and listened for any sounds below.

About ten minutes later, she noticed a new smell seeping into the small room. Smoke. From somewhere below, she detected the smell of something burning. The son of a bitch set the house on fire.

Chapter 40

Panic. A small mewling sound escaped her lips in spite of her intention to stay completely silent. Did he really start a fire? Maybe I'm wrong. Maybe he's still downstairs, smoking a cigar.

As the moments ticked away, the smoke became more apparent. Jadey recognized the smell of burning wood and knew she was in trouble. If this is a ruse to get me to show myself, she thought, it's a pretty good one. She could only stay behind the safe wall for so long as smoke started to billow up around her. She knew, in a fire, most people died from the smoke inhalation. Since she was in an upstairs bedroom, the smoke was rising right up to her.

Jadey quickly reached a point where she had no choice. She had to get out of the house and worried she might have waited too long. Not knowing what waited for her on the other side of the wall, she quietly pulled open the door to the safe room and stepped into her grandma's closet. Already the air was thickening with the smoke, so she pulled a garment from a hanger and held it up to cover her nose and mouth. For an instant, the soft smell of Grandma Ellie's favorite perfume gave her comfort and courage. One hand still clutched the three notebooks to her chest and she stumbled a bit, fearful of the now-distinct hiss and crackle of the flames below. She tried to suppress it, to remain as quiet as she could, but began to cough when the acrid smoke found its way to her lungs.

Caution was no longer an option. She had to get out of the house as fast as she could because she knew the old building would go up fast. Even while she moved toward the stairway, she plotted her exit. Would he be waiting at the back door? The front door? Which would be the quicker exit for her? She looked around for some kind of weapon, but didn't have either the time or a free hand to grab anything in case she encountered him outside. She just had to take the chance and run. She stepped forward and accidentally kicked the work boots she had been wearing earlier, now almost invisible in the dark and smoke. Without pausing, she slipped both feet into them and stepped out of the bedroom doorway.

Jadey almost flew down the stairs and was horrified to see flames engulfing the furniture in the small living room. The fire had already spread from the couch to the curtains. For a second she stared, not believing what she saw, but then her brain refocused on the danger she was in. She had no choice, the only way out was through the kitchen because the flames were starting to curl around the front door.

She had no memory of even turning the knob, because as fast as she could, she barreled through the back door, tripping down the step when her feet couldn't keep up with her zeal to move. Her knee collided with a rock at the edge of a planting bed, sending shooting pain up to her hip. She gasped, both with the pain and with an urgency to draw fresh air into her lungs. Still clutching her grandma's shirt in one hand and the notebooks in the other, she pushed herself up and ran as far away from the house as she could, her knee screaming in pain.

Jadey made it as far back as a row of lilac bushes that formed the edge of the yard, and when she rounded them, she squeezed into the cover of the overgrown shrubs. She forced deep breaths into her lungs, desperate to inhale fresh air and clear her lungs of the smoke, but a coughing fit started and with it came tears pouring from her burning eyes. She used Grandma Ellie's shirt to wipe her eyes and her nose. In the midst of the coughing, she looked back at the house and could see flames through the open back door. No doubt about it, the front room was a total loss.

Was Dent nearby? She still couldn't quite catch her breath. The coughing finally subsided a bit, but her eyes and nose still drained tears and snot. She realized she wouldn't even know if he crept up on her. Finally, after a few minutes of painful breathing and coughing, the breaths started to become easier and the coughing subsided.

Dent must have left as soon as he lit the couch, but the fire had a head start on spreading to other parts of the lower level. The sound of a siren somewhere in the distance reached her ears. A fire truck. Bless Mrs. Sheridan; she must have called 911. As Jadey held the journals close to her breast, she watched the flames devour everything Grandma Ellie worked for.

Chapter 41

The blaze was angry and loud, but the firefighters finally extinguished the flames, and Jadey got a closer look at what remained. The fire reduced the front half of the house to charred hunks of wood and just parts of windows, most of which exploded from the heat. The back half didn't appear to be completely destroyed, but Jadey knew not much could be left worth saving. A small voice in her head scolded her for all of the work she had put in to demolish that kitchen, only to have the fire do a more thorough job in such a short time.

Dawn would be hours away, so the sky exhibited the inky texture that manifests in the middle of the night. It felt like days had passed since she found the skeleton in the shed.

As the firefighters began to store their equipment and coil up the hoses, a car pulled up at the end of the driveway. Jadey didn't recognize the car, and stood frozen to the spot where she watched the flames disappear under showers of pounding water. The door to the unfamiliar blue car opened and Dillanian stepped out, his face registering a myriad of emotions: worry, anger, and determination about something. His eyes met Jadey's, and then he turned to look at the smoking debris.

Jadey cautiously stepped toward him. One side of her wanted to run into his arms, to be held, comforted, told it was going to be all right. The other urged caution. Dillanian worked for Dent. She barely knew him. Did he have anything to do with the evil that was happening in Twin Station?

She stood silently in her sooty cargo pants and t-shirt. Her eyes, red from the stinging smoke and the convulsive coughing, stared at Dillanian, silently questioning his presence. He was out of uniform and driving, she assumed, his own car. He wore blue jeans and boots that looked fit for hiking. An open denim shirt revealed a pale green t-shirt underneath. She felt a little light-headed, as if she were seeing everything through a haze.

Jadey looked up at the dark sky. Her voice was raspy when she spoke, her mind confused, her thoughts scattered.

"It's a completely starless night, Dillanian. Can you see that? A starless midnight. Dr. King talked about that. Why is that?"

Dillanian stared at her, unable to come up with an answer.

"You have to get in my car, Jadey. I have to take you away from here."

She stared at him, as if she didn't understand the language he spoke.

"Jadey, I can't explain it, but I have to get you to safety." He turned to indicate the house. "Look what they're willing to do. You can't stay. Get in my car. I'll take you someplace safe."

Jadey mustered all her courage to speak without allowing the quiver in her voice she knew was right there.

"Are you part of it, Dillanian? Did you do this to me?"

Dillanian's eyes sank. His sorrow was obvious.

"I swear I didn't. I'm not part of it. I can explain it all another time, but for now we need to act fast. Something really big is about to come down and I have to be there to stop it. But first I need to take you someplace. My apartment, or a motel. They're going to keep coming after you."

"Something bigger than burning down my grandma's house while I was hiding inside? It was Dent, you know. I heard his voice. He wanted to kill me."

"I know. It was Dent. And there are a bunch of other people involved. And they're going to do more and I'm afraid maybe a thousand people will die." His voice raised with urgency. "You have to believe me, Jadey."

Jadey looked at her shoes, filthy with soot and dirt.

"I can't go anywhere. I have to see what of my things can be retrieved from the house. This is all I have."

Suddenly conscious of the three notebooks and the shirt she had grabbed from her grandma's closet, she pulled them closer. If Dillanian was part of the scheme, part of the white supremacist group, he'd want to trick her into going with him so he could take the notebooks. Maybe kill her.

But in her gut, she knew that wasn't true. He hadn't even looked at the journals. He had only looked in her eyes, and his own eyes registered real concern. Real pain.

"Prove it to me you're not a part of this."

Dillanian hesitated for a moment, and then went to the trunk of his car and pulled it open. Noticeably, a large duffel bag took up much of the space, but he reached past it into a corner of the trunk, fumbling for something tucked inside a flap. For a second Jadey flinched, as if expecting a weapon in his hand when he brought it back around. Instead, he held a flat wallet, which he slowly opened in front of her. She didn't understand at first. She could see a badge on one side of the flap, and opposite it an ID card. Dillanian's picture was in the middle of the card, and on top, an embossed heading that read "FBI."

Her face twisted with confusion. "FBI? You're not a Twin Station police officer?"

"Undercover. Have been for eight months. I was embedded here because we were investigating a growing vigilante group calling themselves The Clear Order. They're violent, a really fanatical group, and now we're just a day away from their plan to kill hundreds, maybe thousands, at a site I haven't yet identified."

Jadey stood still, trying to absorb what he said. The fog in her brain was clearing.

"Oddly, what you're saying makes sense. I've been reading ...." She squeezed the journals she held in her arms. "I've read some stuff that backs up what you're saying. I'm going with you, whatever you're doing. I want to be there. I can help."

"There is no way that is going to happen." Dillanian led Jadey to his car. He opened the passenger door and she slid in. As he entered the driver's side, he caught her shoving the journals and the shirt under the seat before buckling up.

Her demeanor changed. She was no longer the slightly catatonic young woman who just stood in the driveway next to the house where she almost died. She no longer looked like a victim. Her face was set with determination. She swiped a strand of loose hair out of her eyes.

"You know goddamn well I can't take a civilian along with me. I'll get you someplace safe."

"Forget it Dillanian. Wherever you go, I go. You think you've got something at stake? For you, it's a job. For me, it's my life. They tried to kill me. I just found out they killed my father twenty eight years ago. God only knows what they've done to other people, including maybe my grandma. Now let's go. Time is wasting."

Dillanian looked at her with a mixture of anger and awe. He rolled his eyes and shook his head. But he knew something even Jadey didn't know. Things were happening so fast he didn't have time to take her to a safe place anyway.

Chapter 42

66 Where are we?"

Jadey looked around at the edge of the woods where Dillanian pulled the car to a stop.

"We're about two miles away from the spot I need to intercept them."

The drive took about fifteen minutes and had been all back roads and corn crops. The dark night made it impossible to make out any landmarks. They had entered a more wooded, desolate part of the county, and Jadey found none of it familiar.

Along the way, Dillanian had explained in a short, police-report style recitation, how his undercover work brought to light a year's worth of plans, and suddenly Dent's white supremacist group was green-lit for this weekend. With such short notice, and without knowing the target, Dillanian's back-up team of FBI agents wasn't going to make it before the caravan of heavily armed and very motivated men met up with a like-minded group.

He blamed himself, because even after months of infiltration, Dillanian never cracked the small, inner circle of people that Dent trusted. He knew when Dent tested him, and he consistently talked and acted like he wanted to be let in, but he wasn't local. Dent got to where he was by basically not trusting anyone. As a result, no details ever made it to Dillanian about the location of Dent's target, so without knowing their ultimate destination, and with no back-up on the way, he would do whatever he could to disable the convoy before they ever got started.

He had no intention of bringing Jadey along for this mission.

"You stay with the car. I'm going to hike through these last two miles and make sure those trucks loaded with assault rifles never leave the county."

Jadey looked at him as if he were mad.

"There is no freaking way I'm sitting here in this car. I've got as much of a stake as you do to shut down Dent's operation. People like me are dying, Dillanian. I owe it to them, to my father, to all the ones that may come later, to put an end to this. Right here. Right now."

Dillanian got out of the car and walked around to the trunk, yanking it open. Jadey followed.

"You'll need another pair of hands anyway. You said your back-up wasn't coming, so clearly the plan was never just you against an entire band of assholes. Here, give me that."

Dillanian pulled things from the trunk. He strapped a holstered handgun to his waist and reached for the duffel bag, but Jadey reached in ahead of him and grabbed it.

Beneath the duffel, a rifle with a sling lay on the floor of the trunk. Dillanian pulled it out, racked the bolt back and peered inside. Satisfied, he closed it, put the stock against his shoulder and sighted. His motions were fluid and reflected years of practice with the weapon. Jadey swung the duffel bag over her own shoulder, not even asking what was inside.

When he closed the trunk, Dillanian motioned for Jadey to hand him the duffel. "Let's not argue. Give it to me."

"I agree, let's not argue. Do you have to pee, because there's a tree over there. If not, let's go."

Without waiting for an answer, Jadey headed down the road. Dillanian hung his head with frustration and inevitability. Eventually he looked up and called to her.

"We're not taking the road. We're heading through the woods."

She called back over her shoulder. "I'm liking your choice of the word 'we,' Dillanian. Nice Glock, by the way."

His hand subconsciously touched the holster at his side as he turned to find a break in the trees. Jadey followed close behind.

The going was predictably hard. Clearly no human footsteps got any deeper into these woods than the shoulder when the road was created, so no paths guided them in. The murky night added to the difficulty, although as soon as they entered the woods, Dillanian yanked Jadey to a stop and dug a flashlight from the duffel on her shoulder.

The flashlight was a good one, casting a bright light at least twenty feet ahead of them. Jadey kept close pace to make sure she could see as well as he could, but it didn't stop the occasional whip of a tree branch in her face, or the danger of tripping on uneven ground. Every once in a while, they reached a small clear area where Dillanian searched out the sliver of a moon, as if to gauge direction.

"Was this part of FBI training? Finding your way around a forest with nothing but the moon to guide you?"

"This kind of training I got in the Army. But the FBI does love to drop you off in desolate places, and then challenge you to find your way back."

"Did you come from a family with a law enforcement background?"

"So, we're going to do the 'tell me about your family' thing? Here?"

"You said we have two miles to go. I can't whistle, so talking seems like a decent alternative. You looked ME up. Fair is fair. Spill."

Dillanian sighed as he continued to navigate the thick woods.

"No one else in law enforcement, unless you want to count a brother who was on the opposite side of it. My brother, Kurt, is in Stillwater for blowing up a water tower, destroying thousands of dollars in city property. Watch out for this low branch."

Jadey laughed. "Why did he blow up a water tower?"

"Just to see if he could, I guess. Kurt was never what you would call a 'rule follower.' Gave our mom fits pretty much from the time he arrived in the birthing room. I was ten years old at the time, so with the age difference we didn't exactly hang around each other much growing up. But I should've seen the signs of the kind of people he chose as friends. He'd already been arrested five times before the water tower incident."

Jadey thought about his words for a minute.

"As an only child, I just always blamed everyone else for my problems. No siblings, so it was either my mom, or my grandma, or the kid down the block, or the fire hydrant on the corner. I think my mom would say I gave her fits too."

"I can picture that." Dillanian stopped to turn and look at her. "You've got the look of someone who would give a guy about all he could handle."

He turned back to continue their progress.

"You could find out if you want."

"We're on our way to blow up an ammo dump and you figure this is a good time to flirt?"

"Yes. Should I stop?"

Dillanian paused. Finally –

"No."

Jadey smiled and followed his steps as he and his flashlight found a way through the forest, one step at a time.

Chapter 43

Even in the middle of the night the summer heat barely let up. Coming to a small stream cutting through the forest felt like an oasis. The narrow flow of water meandered through an area with a raised bank on one side, as if eons ago the flow of water had been more like a fast-moving river. Jadey and Dillanian took the opportunity to stop and plan for what was ahead. Jadey scooped up some cool stream water and splashed her face and the back of her neck.

"So, all of that sneaking up at my house, checking me out, asking if I was going to stay – it wasn't because you wanted to get rid of me?"

"I wasn't sneaking. Hell, I rang the damn doorbell the second time."

He looked at her. Then continued.

"I was this close to nailing this bunch and stopping whatever their plan was, and you managed to work your way right into the middle of it. Not on purpose, I know. But there you were and if I didn't stay on top of it, I figured you'd be one of the first casualties. My intent was to warn you off. Get you to back down so I could finish my job."

"Okay, I get that."

"This place we're heading? I've already checked it out on one of my earlier scouting trips. They've got two hundred long guns in boxes. Specifically, Winchester NATO semi-automatics. You're going to see two old metal sheds, and in one they're storing the guns. The boxes of ammo are in the small one. Leading in from I-5, there's a dirt road running through a patch woods, the old driveway to the business that used to be there. On the other side of the sheds is a clearing where they've parked six or seven vans and jeeps for transport."

"What the hell are they going to do with all that firepower? Who are these people?"

"Three of them are right inside of Twin Station PD, including Dent, and I've spent these months documenting their movements and who they mix with. Some of the others are people in town, and in Oakdale. And from the intel I've pulled together, the plan is to meet up with another group coming across from Michigan. They're going to load all of the weaponry into the vehicles from both groups, and head to the site together."

Jadey leaned up against the bank to stretch out her back.

"What site? Who are they targeting?"

"We're not sure yet. They had three targets in their sights, but this weekend is the annual convention of the 'Work of the Angels' group in Chicago. They're expecting as many as three thousand to hear speakers in the common area by the stadium. My best guess is that's ground-zero."

"Work of the Angels? I recognize the name. It's a Black Christian group that organizes specifically to do community work to help poor people. They're the target?

People who help feed and find housing for economically-disadvantaged people? What problem do they have with a group whose mission is peace?"

Dillanian shook his head. "It's not the mission of the group that makes them their target. It's all about the color of their skin. There will be thousands of African-Americans congregating in one small area at a specific date and time."

Jadey clutched her throat as the reality hit her. "It's going to be a bloodbath. So many rifles and nowhere for anyone to run." She turned her face away from Dillanian and didn't notice when he pulled the rifle from his side and put the stock to his shoulder.

"Jay!" he yelled sharply. She turned her face in time to see him pointing the gun at her. For a second everything stopped. Her heartbeat pounded in her ears. She couldn't draw a breath.

"Duck!" was the next thing he yelled, and without thinking she dropped her head and fell to her knees when she felt the bullet whip right past her head. The sound reverberated in her skull as she looked up at Dillanian in shock. *He shot at me! He tried to kill me!*

A movement in the corner of her eye caught her attention and she turned her head back to the bank in time to see a bobcat, a large red stain in the middle of its forehead, crumpling to the ground above her. As she watched, the wildcat continued to slide lifelessly down the side of the hill.

Rocks and dirt, loosened by the large cat's body, followed the progress of the animal down to where it came to rest four feet from Jadey's feet. The rocks loosened other dirt, and it all came to rest on top of the bobcat, half burying it where it lay.

Jadey looked back at Dillanian, stunned. He lowered the rifle and slung it back over his shoulder.

"Good god, that was a fine shot. You kill 'em and bury 'em with one bullet?"

"I've had some training. Are you okay?"

"Besides the fact that my ears are ringing and I thought for a second you were going to kill me, yeah, sure I'm fine."

"He came out of the tree. I didn't even see him until he was almost right on you. You must have looked like a halfway decent meal."

Jadey, still shocked, picked her way over to Dillanian.

"When this is over, I'll make you a gold ribbon to hang on your wall. Wow."

Still a little weak-kneed, she leaned in close to him, glad when he wrapped his arms around her.

"You look a little green around the gills."

"I could use some resuscitation."

He smiled and lowered his head and met her lips with his own. She answered hungrily, reaching up and cupping his face in her hands. Everything was on the line in her life. The police chief coming after her, the notes from her grandma documenting decades of abuse, everything she thought about her hometown had been a lie and, to top it all off, she nearly died as the house burned. She kissed Dillanian with an energy that matched her fear and adrenaline. He returned her passion with the same urgency. Both of their worlds had just flipped over.

Eventually they parted, keeping their faces close, noses almost touching.

"So, what's with the 'Jay' thing? You couldn't manage a simple two syllables?"

"I figured there wasn't enough time to get two syllables out."

She looked at him, her hands still cupping his face.

"Good call."

Chapter 44

Forty-five minutes and arms full of scratches and bug bites later, a break in the forest revealed the camp area, with the weeds around the sheds damp with dew. Dawn was about an hour away, but they could see a hint of lightening on the horizon. Jadey and Dillanian shared a sense of urgency. A quick scan of the nearly two-acre plot revealed they were definitely alone. The two machine sheds stood quietly. The vehicles sat idle. No one milled around.

"I never saw anything with an exact timeline, but we have to move fast. I'm betting they're going to want to get an early start. If I'm right about the target, they'll have about a five-hour drive to Chicago and the event starts tonight at 7:00. They're going to want to get there ahead of time to set up their sniper locations, and they're going to be driving the speed limit the whole way to make sure they don't get pulled over."

"What's the plan here?" We can't load it all into those jeeps and vans and drive away, even if they were dumb enough to leave the keys in them."

"We're not going to move the guns and ammo. We're going to destroy them."

"Huh? Who? How?"

Dillanian reached for the small duffel bag on her shoulder.

"You've been carrying it the whole time. We're going to blow them up."

Jadey jolted and pushed the duffel away from her. "You mean a bomb? I've been carrying a bomb all this time? You have to tell me those things!"

"We don't need a bomb. All of the 'boom' power is already there. We just need to encourage it to go off."

He pulled the zipper and spread the fabric of the duffle bag, showing what he brought.

"Now I know why this thing was so dang heavy." Jadey stared into the bag. "You know that pine resin is flammable, right? We could have just cut a bunch of branches from the pine trees here and got a nice flame going."

"Pine resin is ... what? Are you sure? How would you know that?"

"I had some free time last year and took a few sessions of a master gardening class. Everyone needs a hobby."

"I thought tearing down walls and spackling were your hobbies."

"Those are my superpowers."

Dillanian suppressed a laugh.

"Hey, you just snorted. I heard you. You CAN laugh. Quit hiding it."

"When this place is exploding like the Fourth of July, trust me, I'll be laughing my ass off."

●●●●●

Dent looked around at the eight men assembled next to his car. They arrived at a spot on a dirt road, a mile from the highway, and the nervous energy showed in their stances.

"As I told you, this thing came together really fast after months of planning. The actual place and time weren't decided until about forty hours ago."

Officer Connors stood next to Dent. Even out of uniform their roles as chief and willing subservient was clear. One of the other men spoke up.

"So where are we going? What's the situation?"

Dent cleared his throat to make sure his voice carried all of the strength and authority he wanted to impart.

"We're driving to Chicago, men. We'll be meeting up with our brothers from the White Banner organization at the sheds and from there we'll load up every vehicle we've got with men and arms. But make no mistake. We're in charge of this operation. The Clear Order is supreme here and you, our soldiers, are the finest. All together we expect nineteen men and we have enough arms for each man to carry two long guns and two hand guns, and we've got enough ammo stored for this and the next operation."

Everyone nodded with enthusiasm.

"You've got your backpacks and you'll fill 'em with ammo so you can keep up a continuous reloading procedure. We've practiced for this for a year now. Let's show everyone how well we do our jobs. Connors?"

Connors puffed his chest and cracked his neck side to side.

"Our targets are the sub-humans gathering for the so-called 'Work of the Angels.' They don't know it now, but their real service today will be a symbolic death of the stench they bring to our society. They pretend to worship the same God we do, but there is no room for them here. You know it. They defile our God. They defile our families. They bring down our country with their inte-llectu-al IN-ca-pacity." The last two words were drawn out for sarcastic emphasis.

Dent wrapped it up.

"You're about to go down in history as American patriots. White Banner is due at the sheds in about twenty minutes. We're going to drive in after them, because THAT big moment belongs to us." Dent swept his arm in a wide gesture, mimicking his idol, Adolph Hitler.

●●●●●

Dillanian opened the door of one of the parked jeeps by the machine shed. He pulled down the sun visor and when he didn't find anything he felt under the front seat. His hand came up with a key.

"Our lucky day – they left us the key."

"I suppose they wanted to roll out of here and not worry about some lamebrain forgetting the ring of keys. I'll check the other cars." Jadey headed to the van on the other side of the jeep. A minute later:

"Bingo."

"Pull it around. We're going to park each of them in front of the two doors to the machine sheds." Dillanian drove the jeep to the smaller shed which housed the boxes of ammo. Jadey drove the van to the larger shed and left it there.

"Now for the duffel bag. Those axes are the keys to those two sheds."

Jadey pulled the duffel from her shoulder and unzipped it. Dillanian set his rifle next to the bag and reached in and pulled out a long axe. Removing the protective cover from the blade, he walked over to the chain lock attached to two large metal bolts in the door. Before swinging the axe, he first rattled the chain.

"I was kind of hoping they had just left the lock open for us, like they left the car keys. This is going to take a little more muscle."

"Why didn't you just bring a bolt cutter?"

"Kind of embarrassed to admit it, but I didn't have time to buy one. This thing came up pretty fast."

"But you've got an axe? Who has an axe handy?"

Dillanian looked down at the weapon in his hand. "Everybody? In fact, there are two of them. Back-up."

Jadey took a step back and stared at him.

"How much time do you think we have?" She couldn't help glancing around, as if someone would see them.

"Probably not enough."

"Well then, get to it. I want to see some rippling muscles."

Dillanian looked at her with a shake of the head. "Honey, I'm pretty sure muscles don't ripple. You're thinking of potato chips."

"I'll buy you a big party sized bag of 'em if you break that lock."

"Deal, if it comes with a beer."

Dillanian lifted the axe and brought it down hard on the chain. It rattled a bit, but didn't appear to give at all. Again, he raised the axe above his head and slammed the blade into the chain. This time he saw a bit of a separation between the links, and it spurred him on to hit it again. Sweat beaded on his forehead and, while he continued to work at the first chain, Jadey looked back into the duffel bag.

Good lord, he really did have two of them. She pulled out the second axe and went to work on the other door.

●●●●●

On the dirt road, Doug and Ray Baylor walked back to their car at the end of a line of five others. Doug kept his voice low so only his brother could hear him.

"You know there's a chance none of us is coming back from this. I never heard nothing about an escape plan. We practiced shooting and reloading, but never talked about getting out of wherever we put ourselves. Hell, until right now we weren't even told where we were going."

"I trust Dent to have worked it all out, his brother answered. "And this other group, White Banner? I hear they've been responsible for a couple of the shootings we've seen in the news. They know what they're doing."

Doug stopped by the passenger door of his brother's car.

"That's the problem, Ray. I sure as hell don't know what *I'm* doing. I'm going to admit it, I'm scared as hell. I've got a little girl to think of."

"That'll be the first time you've thought about that little girl. Don't give me any crap about backing out now. You'd embarrass me, Doug. And it's a hell of a long walk back into town from here."

Doug stared at his brother over the hood of the car. His shoulders sagged. His face went pale. He nodded almost imperceptibly and then looked out at the other men waiting expectantly for their orders.

•••••

When Dillanian's axe finally broke through one of the links on the chain barring the door to the machine shed, the entire apparatus fell to the ground. He turned and leaned against the door, wiping his forehead and grabbing the back of his neck. Ten feet away, Jadey was doing her best on the chain that blocked the opening to the other shed that held the ammunition. She turned to look at Dillanian's progress.

"We should have brought a chain saw," she yelled to him.

"Or just drove a ten-ton truck in here and rammed it. Need help?"

"Nope, not a bit. I've got the tiniest little scrape so far in this thick chain. Another hour and a half and I'll be through."

Dillanian smiled and also grimaced as he rocked back on his feet and joined her, dodging the swinging axe.

"Let's alternate. I swing, then you swing?" He looked at her expecting a snappy comeback.

"Sorry, I've got nothing. I'll think of a brilliant retort later. Swing!"

Dillanian lifted the axe above his head and brought it down hard on the chain, at which point the link he hit snapped in half and the chain fell to the ground.

Jadey stared at the door, and then the link on the ground, not believing it was off.

"Show off."

"You loosened it for me."

"I just want to go on the record that I can open all jars of pickles by myself."

Dillanian pulled the double doors open and pushed them wide to reveal the boxes of ammo inside. Then he went back to the machine shed he had been working on and opened those doors wide. Inside were dozens of boxes of Winchester assault rifles, stacked and in rows, ready to be loaded into transport vehicles.

"Now the fun part. We blow them up."

"I see you brought a Firestarter here," Jadey said as she pulled it from the duffel bag. "These things are great for grilling, but you didn't bring an accelerant. I'll remind you of the saga of the pine resin. Do we have time to cut down a bunch of pine boughs?"

"Gasoline. We've got plenty of gasoline." He gestured to the two cars they had parked in front of the sheds.

Motioning for Jadey to step back a bit, Dillanian took a deep breath and then swung his axe at the back-quarter panel of the jeep next to him. After a few hacks, he annoyed it enough that the metal started to pull away from the rest of the car body. Using just his hands, he pulled it farther back, exposing the rear tire and, behind it, the gas tank.

"You're not seriously going to...." Jadey never finished the sentence. Dillanian aimed at the lowest part of the gas tank and swung his axe in an upward motion, striking just above the back wheel. It sunk in a bit and he had to wiggle the axe back and forth to pull it out and ready for another hit. His arms ached with the effort after the pounding on the chains on the doors. One more hit, he thought. Be the lumberjack.

He filled his lungs with air and let it out slowly. Then he drew the axe back and made another huge upward arc, embedding it deep into the gas tank. Immediately gasoline started dripping from the opening and, when he pulled the axe out, gas poured onto the ground and created a little rivulet as it ran toward the shed.

Dillanian looked at Jadey and smiled. "Couldn't have done that with a bolt cutter."

Jadey watched the gasoline snake its way toward the boxes of ammo, mesmerized.

"You know," she said, "King John once brought down an entire castle when he used the fat from forty pigs to slather over the wooden beams. The place went up like a torch."

"I'm only just getting used to these random pearls you come up with. Please don't tell me you learned that in master gardening class."

"I don't remember where I learned it, but sometimes I find some really weird facts in my head."

"I want to know more about what's in that head, but probably later." He grabbed the closest box of ammo and dropped it in the gas rivulet, watching as the box began to soak up the fuel.

"I'm calling this my primer. When this box goes up, everything beyond will get started." He turned to the other parked vehicle. "One more gas tank to smash and we'll douse the guns too."

Just as he was about to swing the axe on the back of the other vehicle by the larger shed, a noise coming from the dirt road caught his attention. Jadey turned too, and saw a line of several cars making their way in to the encampment. A white flag hung from the window of the first in line, with the words "White Banner" in blood red. Jadey looked at Dillanian in desperation.

"Holy shit, they're here. We didn't make it in time."

"We're going to have to skip this gas tank and hope the exploding ammo gets it all." He took the Firestarter from Jadey's hands just as men started emerging from the cars.

●●●●●

Dent reached into his pocket to grab his phone. The buzz indicated an incoming call, and the number on the screen made him smile. He looked at Connors. "This is it. They must be at the sheds."

He put the phone to his ear. "You in?" Dent's face frowned a bit as he listened. "What do you mean? Someone with an axe is what?"

He frowned as he listened to the voice on the other end.

"Holy shit, that's not any one of ours. Stop 'em. Shoot 'em if you have to. We're less than a mile away. Be right there."

•••••

"Take off for the tree line, Jay. Once I light this thing, it's only going to be a short minute before the whole thing starts to go up."

They looked at the men, now standing around their cars, about fifty feet from where Jadey and Dillanian stared at them from the sheds. The guy in the front held a phone to his ear and motioned to those behind him. In one choreographed move, nine guys pulled guns from their waistbands and pointed them at Dillanian and Jadey.

"I'm not kidding, run!" Dillanian yelled as he touched the flame from the Firestarter to the river of gasoline heading toward the boxes of ammunition.

Jadey took off running. The men with guns were now within about forty feet of Dillanian, but the look on their faces revealed uncertainty of what to do. They could see the flames and understood what was about to happen. A couple of them fired shots in Dillanian's direction but at such a long range their accuracy was poor. One of the men yelled caution about shooting anywhere near the river of flowing gas.

Once Dillanian felt satisfied the fire was moving he ran to where Jadey had disappeared into the woods.

The men watched the woman and man run into the woods, and then focused on the trail of flames heading for the shed full of ammunition. In a mad scramble, the White

Banner mercenaries jumped back in their cars, not willing to stick around and get caught in the hellfire.

●●●●●

Dent gripped the phone so hard he almost crushed it. "Shit, shit, shit." He shouted into the phone. "The woods? I know where they are. Dammit, don't leave, we might be able to save this thing." He pulled the phone from his ear when he realized he was talking to air.

Connors saw the fury in his boss's face. "What the hell is going on? They're leaving? We've got a mission!"

Just then, a single explosion happened somewhere through the woods. Connors turned, sudden realization hitting him. "The guns. Our ammo. Someone is blowing it up."

Everyone reflexively hit the ground when the explosions began in earnest. Even from where they were, a mile away, the sound was so furious the line of men waiting by the cars could feel it in their chests. They put their hands over their ears, but it wasn't enough to cover the earth-shattering booms and screaming sounds of metal flying through the air.

Doug had been on the side of the car closest to the woods and now crawled around, the hard gravel cutting into his knees and palms. When he reached Ray, he threw himself down almost on top of him, shouting into his ear. "We've got to get out of here. Let's get in the car and go."

Ray, pressing his hands hard over his ears, shook his head. The explosions were so loud and continuous, he didn't even try to speak.

Chapter 45

Dillanian hit the woods just as the first explosions began and immediately felt shockwaves going through his body from the thunderous pounding behind him. The noise was devastating, and his eardrums seemed nearly about to burst. He pushed through the dense growth, looking for signs of Jadey's direction. All he could do was put one foot in front of the other, ears deafened by the sounds but urging his body to keep going. He hoped Jadey made it deep enough into the woods for some protection in case flying debris came their way.

Suddenly the heat hit his back. The fire behind him was massive, and a quick look over his shoulder revealed flames and flying pieces of parts of the sheds shooting high into the air. The heat burned his eyes and he turned back to continue stumbling through the undergrowth and low branches.

Up ahead he could sense some movement and a flash of color. He pushed harder. One step at a time. Keep going. Keep moving. As he got closer to the source of color, he recognized Jadey's t-shirt.

"Jadey!" He had to yell loudly to be heard over the roar, and the effort made him cough. He couldn't catch his breath and his throat felt raw from the smoke and heat. The second attempt was little more than a whisper. "Jadey."

She sensed his presence and turned to see him storming through the bramble. She stopped in an open area, a spot where it looked as if a camp once stood. Someone cut down trees to create a small area around a long-abandoned fire pit. She sat on a stump to catch her breath.

When Dillanian burst through the woods, she stood and held her arms open. He saw her eyes filled with worry, but she smiled as he came to her. He grabbed her and held on tight, leaning his cheek on the top of her head, and for a few moments they just stood there, holding each other, while the sounds of the explosions gradually began to abate in the background.

"When this is over, I'm going to have to fill out a lot of paperwork."

"I'll help you. I'm a writer. I'll make it sound like something exciting."

He laughed and pulled back and looked at her face.

"I'm glad you're okay. I never would have forgiven myself if something had happened to you."

"I never would have forgiven you if you hadn't come to find me."

Jadey stood on her tiptoes. She kissed his neck and then his chin, and then met his lips as he lowered his face to hers. After a moment, they stood together, looking back at the fireworks when a voice behind them made them jump.

Chapter 46

“I admit you had me fooled, Dillanian. I would have figured her for this, but not you. What turned you?”

Jadey and Dillanian spun to face Howard Dent, surrounded by eight other men. Seven of the men pointed guns at them. Jadey looked at the group and gasped when she recognized Doug, whose head was down, hands in his pockets.

“Give it up, Dent. It’s over.” Dillanian managed to put emphasis in his voice, in spite of the effects of inhaling caustic smoke.

“It’s not over until I say it’s over. I admit you dealt us a bit of a setback, Dillanian, but we’ve been around for a long time. You’ve never seen a group of people more determined to get back what’s theirs. Many have died as heroes to take back our country. I expect more will again.”

Jadey’s eyes bore into Dent’s. “Any of them come back from a fire meant to kill them Dent? See many other ghosts recently?”

Dent was silent, shifting his feet. Connors spat on the ground and spoke up.

“You know, it’s a shame. I kinda figured I’d have a go at you at some point. I mean, I’d take a shower afterward in case any of that melatonin stuff rubbed off, you know.”

He laughed at his joke and a couple of his thugs laughed behind him.

Ray Baylor spoke up, addressing his comment to Dent. "Chief, the fire." He nodded his head in the direction of the explosions. It was quieter now, except for an occasional single bang, but the sizzle of the fire remained, and it became apparent the woods had caught.

Jadey bore her eyes into the top of Doug's head, willing him to look at her. How could he be a part of this? When did he become a terrorist? Look at me, she thought. Talk to me. Doug – who did you become?

Dent recognized the urgency of the fire and stared again at Dillanian and Jadey, giving clear instructions to his men.

"We're going to let the fire take 'em. Seems like a fitting end considering the damage they've done. Let the roasting of their own flesh be the last thing they know."

He turned to Doug, who still had not lifted his face.

"I'm going to give you the honors, Baylor. Prove yourself, right here. Show us you've become a man today." Doug looked up with horror on his face. His eyes finally found Jadey's, and tears threatened to form as he looked at his old friend.

"Connors, get him a couple of lengths of rope and let him tie them up. Wendell, relieve Officer Dillanian of his gun."

Doug started to back away, but the others in the group pushed him forward. Connors handed him two lengths of rope and smirked at him. Doug looked directly at Ray, hoping for some help. His brother looked back at him, no mercy in his face.

"You've got to do this, Doug. This is our life, our country, our people. Do it or we'll leave you here too."

"Ray? Why? What's happened to you?"

Ray just looked away. Connors shoved Doug.

As Doug approached Dillanian, the FBI agent reached out to grab him, but three of the armed men planted themselves a foot away, handguns pointed at Dillanian's head. One of them pulled the handgun from Dillanian's holster. Connors goaded him from the sidelines.

"Go ahead and make a move Dillanian. It'll be quicker for you, but you're probably a coward anyway. Not much of a co-worker, that's for sure."

Laughs erupted from the group. Dillanian looked at the barrage of guns pointed at him and relented. They pushed him up against a tree and held his arms behind it while Doug wrapped the length of rope around his wrists. He began the process almost gently, but harassment from the other men made Doug pull harder, yanking the rope between Dillanian's wrists and wrapping the ends through the loops. With a final hard tug, the knot set. Doug stepped away.

Jadey looked at the tree next to Dillanian and at the men with the guns. "You can put down your guns, cowboys. You're all holding them wrong anyway."

For a second they looked confused, and then resumed their stance. Doug gently pulled Jadey to the tree and she put her hands back around the tree for him. She heard him sniffle and barely heard his whispered words. "I'm sorry, Jadey."

The other men took the opportunity to give Dillanian a couple of kicks. Given more time, they'd have beat him unconscious, but they watched the progress of the fire and were eager to get moving. They left Doug alone with Jadey, and he was gentler with her, wrapping the rope around her wrists but not yanking them as tight. After multiple twists and winding of the rope through the binds, he did something that startled her. He pulled her fingers down, opening her hand, and then shoved the ends of the rope in it. Then he closed up her fingers around the rope, gave her hand a quick squeeze, and stepped away from the tree. Without a word, he went back to the other members of The Clear Order and stood with his back to Jadey and Dillanian.

"Now that wasn't so hard, was it, Dougie?" Dent goaded him. Most of the rest of your old school friends will still be alive when this is all over. Go have a beer with them later."

Dent looked up to watch the pace of the fire, slowly gaining on them.

"Let's head back to the cars, men, or we'll all get caught in this fire. We're only sacrificing two lives today."

Jadey turned to look over at Dillanian as the sounds of the retreating men disappeared into the woods. He already started to struggle against the ropes holding him, wincing as they cut into his wrists. She let her own hand open a bit and used the fingers from her other hand to pull on the ends of the rope tucked into her hand. She gently tugged on them, careful not to let them fall out of her reach. After a few tugs, she felt the rope around her wrists loosen a bit.

"Dillanian, I think Doug tied mine with a slip knot. He handed me the ends, and when I pull on them it's loosening, just a bit."

Dillanian looked over, craning his neck to try to see her hands. "Keep pulling. You're right, it doesn't look like a real knot."

She carefully slid her fingers further up on the length of rope and pulled again. Her hand ached from the twisted position this caused, but she pulled hard, suddenly feeling the binding go slack. Buoyed by the progress, she picked up the pace, pulling on the loose ends, but then caught a glimpse of the woods in front of them.

"The fire. It's moving fast."

"Focus on the knot. Keep pulling. I can see it loosening."

The heat of the fire was now making them sweat. Both of them closed their eyes against the blasts of wind that brought dancing embers into the space around them. Jadey continued to work the rope until finally the last twist pulled free and the rope dropped to the ground.

"I didn't think Doug could've helped them kill me."

"Well, he apparently didn't feel the same about me because my knot is tied tight as shit."

Jadey quickly worked on the knot that was digging into Dillanian's wrists. It was tied tight, and her fingers, so sore from the pounding with the axe, the heat, and from fighting on her own knot, wouldn't work at first. She couldn't get them to separate the twists of the rope. "Dammit, my fingers...."

"That fire looks hungry, honey. See what you can do."

She spoke to her fingers. "Work, come on. If you can type a four-hundred-page manuscript you can untie a damn knot!"

The heat became almost unbearable. The skin on her arms felt as if it were curling up. Each second brought more heat, and she could only imagine how Dillanian felt on the other side of the tree, facing the oncoming fire. What was it about fire? Twice in two days? She'd probably never roast another marshmallow in her life.

"Work it. Work it. This is loosening. Come on, pull it through. Why did Doug make so many twists? Dammit!"

Finally, a loop she pulled loosened the rope enough so Dillanian could yank at it himself. The cutting of the rope made his wrists bloody, but he kept working until the entire tangle was loosened enough for him to pull his hands free.

Dillanian grabbed Jadey's hands and pulled her from the advancing fire and into the other side of the woods.

"Wait! This is the way they went. They'll see us."

"No choice. We've got to get as far away from the fire as we can. We can hope they've driven away by now, but this is our only way out. I'm betting their cars were all parked on the dirt road that breaks off from the highway."

The movement of the group of men had created a bit of a path for them, with fewer thickets and low branches to slow their pace, but they still fought against the whiplash of tree branches and sharp briar bushes. Eventually they distanced themselves from the fire enough for the intense heat to lessen slightly. They slowed their pace a bit, a little more cautious about what was ahead of them. Dillanian rubbed his sore wrists against his shirt and watched Jadey's back as she pushed her way through the narrow path ahead. His face dropped in horror when he saw an arm reach out and yank Jadey into the undergrowth.

Chapter 47

Before he could move, Jadey emerged again, with Connors right behind her. His left arm held her back up tight against his chest. His right hand held a gun to the side of her head.

"I took a guess that young Baylor wouldn't do a particularly good job of tying you two up. I hate it when I'm always right." He smiled without humor, his black eyes boring into Dillanian's.

Dillanian's face was grim. He looked at Jadey's face and could see she was coiling to fight. He tried to catch her eyes and warn her off.

"You haven't killed anyone yet, Connors. There's still time to make this right."

"You don't understand, Dillanian. I was prepared to kill a thousand people today, and I know my God would have blessed me for it. So, to kill just two would barely create a blip."

Jadey tilted her head against his chest to try to look up at him. "You think God wants you to murder innocent people? Are you sure you don't have Him confused with Satan?"

Connors tugged her closer, causing her to gasp for breath when his arm compressed her lungs.

"They're not innocent when they've come to this land with the purpose of taking what is rightfully ours. People like you, stained by the sins of the mutants from Africa. They think they've settled in here to take over, but we'll take 'em out one at a time if we have to."

He leaned in close to Jadey's ear and whispered with a hoarse croak, Jadey's stomach lurching from his foul breath. "But we like it better when we can wipe 'em out in herds. More efficient, right?"

Jadey reacted with a sudden retching motion, gulping for air, twisting a little as if she was about to throw up. Connors unconsciously lightened his grip around her shoulder, and in that second Jadey jammed her right fist straight up under the wrist of the hand holding the gun. The instant spasm in his wrist loosened his hold. The gun flew into the air and land on the ground three feet in front of them.

Before Connors could blink, Dillanian picked up the gun and now pointed it at Connors, who retightened his grip on Jadey.

"Let her go."

Connors laughed.

"Why, so you can shoot me?"

"I don't want to shoot you; I want to arrest you. Let her go."

"You know I don't need a gun to kill her. It would only take a second to snap this little brown neck."

"If you kill her, you no longer have a hostage and you're a dead man."

"People like me are willing to die for their cause. How about you, Dillanian? Are you willing to die today?"

For a moment no one spoke. Dillanian's eyes bore into Connors.

"Remember the bobcat!" Jadey's whispered voice broke the brief silence.

Dillanian looked at her, confused, and then understood what she meant. No, he thought, panicking. Don't try it. He gave his head a shake to stop her.

She started counting. Connors screwed up his face, confused by her voice, her counting.

"One ... two ... THREE!" At 'three' she dipped her head down as far as she could, pushing hard against Connors' left arm where he held her tight across her chest. At the same time, she heard the single 'pop' of a gunshot. For a second, she thought Dillanian must have missed because Connors' grip remained tight. But then, almost in slow motion, she felt him falling back, taking her down with him, his arm still heavy against her body.

With a thud, they landed on the ground, Connors flat on his back and Jadey on top of him. The arm that had held her now lay lifeless on the ground. She scrambled up as fast as she could and stepped away before looking back. A single bullet hole distorted the center of his forehead. His open eyes saw nothing.

"Oh geez, oh man," Jadey squealed as she reached Dillanian, who still held the gun pointed at Connors. She stepped behind him and peered over his shoulder at the prone body.

"He's dead, right? He's not going to move, right?"

Dillanian finally lowered the pistol and turned to her, wrapping his arms around her.

"You idiot. What if I missed?"

"I knew you wouldn't. I saw you shoot a moving bobcat, but only after you yelled for me to duck. I just ducked again."

He held her for a moment. He kissed the top of her head.

"More paperwork, right?" She looked up at his face.

"I'll be swimming in paperwork. You all right?"

She nodded. "Let's keep moving. The fire is still coming after us. You said there's a dirt road ahead?"

"Yeah. It's from an old logging road. Cuts through between Highway 5 and the county road. It's where I'm guessing they parked when they came through the woods like they did."

With renewed adrenalin, they shoved the overgrowth aside and charged through the woods, always aware of the fire behind them and the possibility Dent and the others were still ahead. After several minutes, they could hear voices ahead, so they stopped, listening.

Dent's voice was recognizable. "Where the hell is Connors? Did he stop to piss and get lost?"

Another voice spoke up. "Want me to go back and find him?"

"No," Dent answered. "I want *six* of you to go back and find him. I got a feeling something's wrong and I want all our firepower aimed at it. Get your guns out of your cars and go back in, two at a time."

Dillanian looked at Jadey and spoke directly into her ear, to keep his voice as low as possible.

"I have to stop them before they get to those guns. Stay here."

He slowly crept forward, the handgun in front of him, and when he emerged from the woods, he had it aimed directly at Dent. Dent's men, having just turned to get to their cars, were all fanned behind him, watching. Only Dent was armed, a handgun held by his side.

"Well, if it isn't the master explosives expert. Again. I don't remember reading about that in your papers when you applied for the job. Let me guess. ATF?"

"FBI," replied Dillanian. And I've got five cars of agents heading this way right now. Make this easy, Dent. You only conspired to commit terrorism; you haven't done it yet. Don't make this any worse."

"Where's Connors?"

"Connors isn't coming."

Dillanian's words hung in the smoky air.

Dent said nothing but his eyes revealed a slight hesitation. Was it fear? The expression lasted a second, just a flicker, and then his eyes shifted to look behind Dillanian.

"I see you brought the little lady with you. Now how did you both manage to get out of those ropes? Did you have a little help?"

He turned to look where Doug Baylor stood, calmly raised the gun in his hand and shot. Doug's eyes registered shock as the force of the bullet pushed him back. He clutched a bloody chest as he landed, already dead. Dent calmly turned back, the gun back at his side.

"Doug!" Jadey screamed. "Oh my god. You bastard!" She glared at Dent, wanting to lunge at him but wary of the gun at his side. "You sick bastard!"

At the same time Dillanian tightened the grip on the gun he had aimed at Dent. He yelled as loud as he could. "Put the gun down, Dent. Put the fucking gun down!" Dent calmly tossed the gun into the space between them and stared at Dillanian.

Behind Dent, the remaining men looked unnerved. They hadn't signed up for this, and Doug was their friend. Ray looked down at his brother in shock.

"He never really had what it took to be one of us. I probably would have shot him and left him behind in Chicago if we had made it there. And speaking of that, our comrades are probably due here any second. You may want to hightail it while you still have a chance."

"They're not coming either, Dent." Dillanian stood his ground. "They couldn't get out of the clearing fast enough. By now they're all stopping for a change of underwear before they head back to the holes they came from. What they don't know is FBI agents will be all over them before this day is over. You're all out of friends, Dent."

Dillanian still had his gun trained on Dent and, at twelve feet away, Dent knew Dillanian wouldn't miss. Dent showed an air of composure, not confrontation.

"You can have us all arrested by your FBI friends, Dillanian, but you know I'll walk. You've got nothin' on me, or any of us. We just stopped our cars when we saw some explosions. Hell, we were all just going out to breakfast together."

"How about murder?" Dillanian nodded his head toward Doug's body. He heard Jadey stifle a sob behind him.

"He accidentally shot himself. That's what all of my men saw. That's what they'll testify."

No one behind Dent spoke, but the men shuffled their feet, antsy, uncertain, agitated.

Jadey took a step closer to the chief. "Have you told your men about your own Black ancestry, Dent?" Jadey choked out the words, not able to hide the sob that stuck in her throat, her eyes darting between Dent and Doug's body on the ground.

Dent looked at her, tilting his head. "Are you speaking English girl? What ancestry are you talking about?"

Jadey looked at the men standing behind Dent, her eyes making sure she had their attention. Ray moved closer to Doug's body, and then knelt down next to it.

"I do a lot of research for my writing, and got curious about your own ancestry. I'm sure people have noticed over the years you're a bit ... let's call it 'dark-complected'. I suppose you've told them you came from Spanish ancestry, or something. Maybe Italian. It's kind of a wonder what those ancestry sites can tell you these days."

Dent turned to his men. "Get those guns from your cars. He can't shoot us all."

"Trying to change the subject, Dent? Afraid if they hear the truth about you, they'll run?"

She directed her comments to Dent's followers, who now stared at the back of Dent's head.

"I'm betting he never told you. Your chief's five-time great grandma was a woman named Mayebelle Woodson. The last name was borrowed from her owner, because that's how slaves got last names in those days."

Low mumbling sounds came from the crew, as some of the men whispered, others even chuckling. Dent turned to them.

"You're not listening to her, are you? There's no Mayebelle in my family! Never would be a slave in my background. Hell, my ancestors would have been the slave *owners*."

He turned back to Jadey with a smug smile, but his eyes showed a speck of doubt.

"And there are pictures," Jadey went on as if there had been no interruption. "She was a fine-looking woman, but boy, she had to live in a rough little hovel, just next to the plantation. Not a great place to raise a child who was half Black and half White. But you're partly right, Dent. At least one of your ancestors was no doubt the slave owner."

"Ridiculous. You're just making this up. No one here is even listening to you. Go back to that pile of rubble house of yours."

Jadey continued. "According to the ancestry sites, the child ended up marrying White, so the generations started to get lighter and lighter. Pretty soon they were able to pass, and by then Lincoln freed the slaves and no one was any the wiser. Think about it Dent. You carry African heritage in your blood. Your father had an even greater share. And that favorite grandmother you spent time with as a child? She had an even greater share."

Jadey stared at Dent with eyes hardened by the man's own evil. "Were you going to tell your men, Dent? Were you ever going to reveal to them the family secret, that you are actually the same as the people you were going to kill?"

Now Dent was furious, and he looked around him, lashing out. "Bullshit. Bullshit, I say. Let's finish this right here. Right now."

The men looked at each other and didn't move. Ray Baylor cradled Doug's body, and then picked him up in his arms and started back to his car, not saying a word, not looking at anybody. Jadey's eyes followed him, tears welling at the corners.

Dent ignored the Baylors and shouted at the remaining wannabe soldiers.

"Remember the mission. It's all about the mission. You're not going to let some half-blood turn you against everything you've ever wanted. Think about your families."

"Half-blood. Like you, Dent?" Jadey practically spit out the words.

Dent turned to Jadey, furious. He took one step toward her but eyed the gun Dillanian had trained on him, and stopped. Then he smiled again, a smile that told a tale of fury mixed with self-satisfaction. He had one more card to play.

"Speaking of family, little bitch, your grandma sure was a handful. She actually put up a bit of a fight when I went to her house that day. I planned to push her down the stairs and let the stairs kill her, but she was way too feisty. So I snapped her neck first, and then tossed her down like a rag doll."

He puffed up his chest as if he had just declared himself king. Jadey let out a howl emanating from the center of her belly, and the look on her face bordered on madness. The sound from her was animal-like, and she charged at Dent, surprising him with her speed and ferocity. Her eyes reflected pure fury as she launched her small body against the enormous police chief.

The force of her momentum, and the element of surprise, caught him with uneven footing, and she pushed him backward as hard as she could. Awkwardly trying to catch his balance, he swung his arms around, and crashed backward into his parked car. His head hit the bumper of the vehicle hard and he went down, unconscious.

Around him, no one moved. Jadey stood where she made contact with him, her hands on her knees, her head tilted in Dent's direction, ready if he made a run at her. But he didn't move. His chest rose and fell, so she knew he was alive, but he lay crumpled next to his car.

Eventually, one by one, the others all quietly walked toward their cars. Dillanian followed their movements with his eyes on them and his hands on his gun, but they were in no mood for a firefight. They got into their cars and drove away.

Chapter 48

By the time the back-up from the FBI arrived, Dillanian and Jadey had tied the hands of the now-groggy, but awake Dent. Dillanian stood with the other agents and summarized the events of the last few hours. Jadey stood over the place where Doug fell, his blood mixing in with the dirt and an impression where his head hit the ground.

She didn't see Dillanian join her, but she felt his arm go around her shoulder and pull her close.

"You were amazing there, honey. I can't believe you had time to do all of that research on Dent. He couldn't believe it either."

"Research? Don't forget, Dillanian, I write fiction for a living. Sometimes I just make shit up."

He hugged her. I think it's about time you started calling me Greg."

Chapter 49

Jadey stood in front of her grandma's house one last time. The fire left the front of the house charred and most of the roof missing. Burned boards jutted from the structure, and what was left of the furniture inside was almost unrecognizable.

The back of the home fared better, but just barely. Through the gaping openings in the front, Jadey saw what remained of the staircase, and vaguely wondered if the third step still creaked. The thought of it brought back the night of the fire with Dent creeping up those stairs, and the frightening, eerie sound when he hit the third step. She shuddered and looked away.

The fire had been six days ago, but she thought she could still smell the smoke in her hair. Eight or nine showers back at her mom's place, and she still imagined every strand smelled of wood smoke.

The sound of a car approaching drew Jadey's attention away from the house. Her tense shoulders eased when she saw Dillanian's face through the windshield. She watched him open the door and ease his legs onto the driveway. She remembered her first sighting of him, stopped behind her in his patrol car, and those long legs emerging from the door.

His face was grim as he gazed at the house, but then softened when he looked at Jadey. She stood by her car, the trunk open. The few things inside barely filled the well of the trunk.

"Did the fire chief get you inside?"

"Yep. There were only a few places safe enough to walk. He took me through, but didn't let me linger much. I scavenged some photos, which was nice. Not much else."

"When you arrived in town, your back seat and trunk were so loaded down I'm surprised you didn't scrape the pavement all the way here."

She smiled at the memory. Was that only three weeks ago?

"I couldn't figure out the proper way to stand by my car to flag down help. Was my 'come on' look too much?"

"I'd say it was just about right. But I would have stopped if you were eighty, balding, and held a sign saying 'please don't stop.'"

"I'm glad it was you that day."

He stared at her.

"I took one look at you, Jadey Orion Evans, and couldn't stop thinking about how goddamn beautiful you were. Not very professional, I admit."

Jadey smiled. "I won't tell anyone. You probably figured from that kiss in my kitchen that I had similar thoughts about you."

Her gaze returned to the house.

"I think I've seen enough here to fill another book, but I decided I'm going to leave it to my friend Lynn to write."

"Have you seen Katie at all?"

"She won't talk to me. She walked away from me at Doug's funeral. I'm sure she blames me for her boyfriend, Dent, ending up on the wrong side of a jail cell. I'm going to give it a couple of weeks and then try to call her. She's hurting too."

"Any regrets?"

Jadey thought about it for a minute.

"Maybe one. When I launched myself at Dent, wouldn't it have been cool if I had been screaming at the top of my lungs, 'It's clobbering time!'?"

She gazed at him. His eyes smiled. He offered his take.

"It would have made the moment more interesting."

She laughed.

"How's the paperwork going?"

"Maddening, but they're giving me time to finish. This town's going to have a lot of work ahead of it. The whole police department needs to be revamped. Three of the uniforms are going to prison. You're going to love that your grandma's journals have been a goldmine of information. You'll get the originals back when they're done with them, and there'll be more arrests before the investigation is done."

Jadey smiled and looked off toward town.

"You know who they were going to kill, Dillanian? They were going to murder people who are raising their children with the same hopes and dreams everyone has. They were going to kill people who take their aging parents to baseball games. They're people who read the Sunday comics and laugh out loud at them. They have family holiday gatherings where they sing songs together, and tease each other about what they got for them last Christmas. They teach their kids to drive, keeping one hand on the dashboard and one foot planted firmly on the floor, searching for that invisible second brake. They watch them become independent. They encourage them to go to a trade school, or college. They cry at their weddings."

Dillanian nodded. Silent.

"Thinking of quitting the FBI to take the police chief job here?"

"Nope. I've put in for a transfer to the Minneapolis FBI office."

Jadey's face lit up. She couldn't believe how pleased she felt.

"Funny, with my house reduced to ash here, I'm transferring back to Minneapolis too."

They stared at each other.

"Tell me, FBI guy, do you come with any baggage?"

"I have both checked-in and carry-on. How about you?"

"Ditto. How do you feel about a woman with a skeleton in her shed?"

"You mean closet?"

"No, in this case I mean shed, which survived the fire. You won't believe who's in it."

THE END

About the Author

Lynn Garthwaite is the author of the Dirkle Smat Adventure four-book series, written especially for first and second grade reading levels. She has also written picture books for clients, including Radio Flyer and Shutterfly, and an historic non-fiction titled *Our States Have Crazy Shapes: Panhandles, Bootheels, Knobs and Points*. In addition to the printed book world, she has written seven screenplays, still hoping to one day see them produced. Lynn is an award-winning producer and co-host of the cable TV show "That's Odd" and a committee member for the annual WOW Women of Words Writers' Conference. Lynn lives in Bloomington, MN with her husband and a big garden.